DRUG LORD:

PART 2

Detective Damien Drake

Book 7

Patrick Logan

Books by Patrick Logan

Detective Damien Drake

Book 1: Butterfly Kisses

Book 2: Cause of Death

Book 3: Download Murder

Book 4: Skeleton King

Book 5: Human Traffic

Book 6: Drug Lord: Part 1

Book 7: Drug Lord: Part II

Chase Adams FBI Thrillers

Book 1: Frozen Stiff

Book 2: Shadow Suspect

Book 3: Drawing Dead

Book 4: Amber Alert

Book 4.5: Georgina's Story

Book 5: Dirty Money

Book 6: Devil's Den

Dr. Beckett Campbell Medical Thrillers

Book 0: Bitter End

Book 1: Organ Donor

Book 2: Injecting Faith

The serpent is helpless unless he finds an apple to work with.

–George Ade

.

Prologue

NOBODY SPOKE ENGLISH. EVEN THE captain of the vessel, who was purportedly from Illinois, spoke in a strange dialect that Drake could barely understand.

Spanish, Portuguese, and some sort of hillbilly backwoods talk filled Drake's ears for the better part of the voyage from New York City to Riohacha. Under normal circumstances, this would have annoyed him to no end, but not now. Now, he didn't mind being alone. In fact, part of the reason he was making this journey by himself was because he wanted to be alone.

Being unable to communicate with others meant that there was no burden to explain things that he barely understood himself. The only downside of this was that Drake spent a lot more time in his own head. He thought about Clay a lot, thought about all the fucked-up things that had happened since his friend had been killed. He also thought about his son, whom he'd met only for a few minutes, and then about Jasmine, the woman he still loved despite finding out that she was involved in the smuggling ring.

But most of the time, Drake thought about Ken; Ken Smith, the true Skeleton King.

I was so close… so goddamn close.

Everything Drake had been through since Clay's murder had led up to the confrontation in Ken's penthouse apartment. All of the betrayals, all of the pain and suffering, the death, would have been worth it if Drake had just been a little faster, if he'd managed to nab Ken.

But the slimy bastard had slipped away, retreating to the only place where he still had people he trusted.

The place where he imported his heroin from.

The fact that Drake had finally ensnared Raul and that Sgt. Yasiv was in the process of pressing charges against all the crooked cops on Ken's payroll, was *mildly* satisfying.

But it wasn't enough.

Drake *needed* Ken, maybe even more than he needed to know what happened to his brother.

"*¿Estas buscando a alguien?*"

Drake lifted his eyes and stared at the Colombian man standing before him. He had tanned skin and a wide nose. His black hair was dry in places and puffy in others as if he'd selectively washed only random sections of it. Like Drake, the man's face was covered in sweat and moisture from the sea, and his clothes were filthy.

"*¿Quieres un trago?*"

He was holding a bottle of liquor out to Drake and he instinctively reached for it. A moment before he grabbed the bottle, however, Drake hesitated.

It wasn't that he didn't want the liquor; despite the captain's promise of copious amounts of booze on board, they'd run out in only a day or two. It was the man's timing that Drake found curious; they were only a day out now, maybe less depending on the sea, and not once had any of the five Colombian below deck said a single word to him before now.

They hadn't bothered trying to introduce themselves, they didn't offer Drake anything that they had brought with them on board, nor had they even acknowledged him.

Drake wasn't offended; you had to do something fairly reprehensible to smuggle yourself *into* Colombia and keeping to yourself was something to be expected.

"*¿Beber?*" the man asked, this time sloshing the bottle for effect.

Drake, for one, was on the hunt for the man responsible for bringing carfentanyl-laced heroin into New York. A powerful, violent man with connections, a man capable of murder. In an ideal situation, Drake would arrive in Colombia, deal with Ken, and slip back out again without upsetting any drug lords in the process.

But nothing that Drake had done over the past few years could be described as ideal.

"Fuck it," he said, reaching for the bottle.

The liquor was some sort of over proofed rum, and Drake could only manage two long pulls before the burn was too great. He wiped his mouth with the back of his sleeve and then handed the bottle back.

"My name's Drake," he said, knowing full well that the man probably didn't understand a word of what he was saying. "And I needed that."

"Drake?" the man asked, shaking his head. "No, I don't think so."

Drake was so taken aback by the man's nearly flawless English that he simply gaped.

"No, you're not Drake," the Colombian said, still shaking his head. "You are *el phantasmo;* you, my friend, are a ghost."

PART I

The Survey

Somewhere near Dibulla, La Guajira
COLOMBIA

1984

Chapter 1

"I BET YOU DIDN'T THINK you were going to be doing this after Operation Eagle Claw," Ken Smith said as he tucked a wad of chew into his lower lip. He jammed it in deep with his tongue and then spit some residue off his lips. "Going from trying to free US hostages in Iran to babysitting a couple science nerds, did you?"

When the man across from him didn't answer, Ken looked up. Cpl. Carl Weathers was staring off into the distance, his dark eyes focused on something that Ken couldn't see. He was dark-skinned, with even darker lines around his mouth which he tried to hide with a goatee. He looked much older than he had back when they'd been partners during Eagle Claw, even though that was less than a year ago. He looked older, and as his name suggested, *weathered*.

Ken leaned forward and spat a wad of brown tobacco juice near Carl's shoe.

"That was close," the man said absently.

"Close only counts in horseshoes and hand grenades. Did you hear anything that I said?"

Weathers' eyes drifted back to the horizon and Ken followed his stare.

Colombia *was* beautiful, Ken had to give her that. Sure, the country was host to a whole shit ton of problems, but she was beautiful. And this beauty seemed to only increase the more distance they put between themselves and civilization. Out here, the lush vegetation was greener, the canopy of trees above denser, the persistent bird calls more... well, *persistent*.

It was also *hot*.

Ken reached up and wiped his forehead with his arm, which proved ineffective; both were slick with sweat. The sun had barely broken the horizon and yet his camo shirt was already clinging uncomfortably to his back and chest.

"Goddamn birds," Weathers whispered. "Will they never shut up?"

Ken wondered what had gotten into his friend; he'd gone from distant to ornery in a matter of hours. They'd been on Colombian soil now for three days, following around the six scientists from RAND Corporation taking their bullshit surveys. Both he and Carl were fully strapped, but there was little chance that they'd be using their guns on this trip. It was bullshit, all of it—political meanderings. The locals they came across were all smiles, even going as far as to offer them glasses of their horrible local moonshine.

Ken easily saw through this facade; they were placating them, pretending that there was no drug problem here. They told RAND whatever lies would send the scientists and their US soldier buddies back home the quickest.

And Ken didn't blame them, nor did it bother him. He was getting paid and getting paid well to protect these six scientists and their precious surveys. After their botched mission in Iran, this was a walk in the park. Besides, First Sergeant Loomis had suggested that this was just a step to bigger and more lucrative things. And with two little ones at home, Ken knew that—

"I've got a bad feeling about this," Weathers said suddenly.

Ken rolled his eyes.

"Let me ask you something, Weathers."

The man turned to look at Ken.

"You ever get a *good* feeling about anything? Like, when you're fucking your wife, right before you're gonna come, do you whisper in her ear, *I've got a bad feeling about this*?"

Carl Weathers' lined face twitched a little, which made Ken grin. This was the most emotion he'd gotten out of the guy in days.

"Yeah," Ken said with a chuckle, "I bet you do. I fuckin' bet you do."

Ken wondered briefly if he'd have traded some of the man's loyalty for a tiny splinter of a sense of humor. In Iran, Carl's unwavering resolve and concentration were paramount in them getting out of there alive. But here?

Just a goddamn grin, please.

"Naw," Weathers muttered, as he started to move toward their makeshift base camp. "I only say that when I'm fucking *your* wife."

Ken's eyes bulged, and he froze mid-step, watching his friend walk away from him. Carl was a hair over six feet tall and a solid two-hundred and twenty pounds. And his dark black skin, now glistening with sweat, made every one of those pounds of muscle stand out.

"Wait!" Ken hollered, as he started after his friend. "Carl... *stop!* I think... I think you have heat stroke."

When Carl turned back to look at him, a frown on his face, Ken grinned broadly.

"You... you made a joke! Maybe you should lie down, Carl, 'cuz heat stroke is serious business."

Chapter 2

"IN A COUPLE YEARS, TEN, tops, you mark my word; all the drugs in the US are going to be coming out of Mexico, not Colombia," Weathers stated as he hacked his way through more shrubbery. In addition to the useless RAND scientists, they had two guides with them, locals who had agreed to lead them through the jungle to their final village for a pocketful of change. Anything to get them out of Colombia faster Ken supposed. Still, armed with moderately dull machetes and fueled by local moonshine, Ken and Carl took the front position.

Ken swiped his blade at a mangrove sapling, shearing it clean off. It was sweltering out now—balls sticking to the inside of your thighs hot—making Ken regret wearing such thick clothing. It was supposed to protect him from insects, but he'd gratefully take a dozen bee stings just to cool down a few degrees.

He had no idea how the six nerdy scientists behind them dressed in long shirts and khaki pants of all things were surviving. They truly were a strange breed.

"It's true," Weathers continued without provocation. "You know, after the last war on drugs shut down the Cuba-Miami shipping route, Colombia started using Mexico as a go-between. They have no problem getting their drugs *into* Mexico, and from there they just hijack the established methods for moving marijuana to move their heroin and cocaine into the US."

Ken hacked his way up next to Carl.

"Why do we even care, that's what I want to know," Ken said absently. Weathers stopped swinging his blade and turned to look at him. His face was glistening with sweat, making it almost shine.

"Why do we care? These drugs are killing people, man. Even pot… it's a gateway drug. My brother had a friend who started smoking weed…"

Ken stepped in front of his friend as he spoke, hacking away at more saplings. He'd heard this rhetoric before, of course, of pot being a gateway drug, about the perils of addiction. But none of this changed the most basic issue at hand.

"Yeah, well, if someone wants to put poison in their body, who am I to tell them differently?" Ken offered when Carl paused to catch his breath. "Who is anybody to tell them differently?"

"The US government, that's who," Weathers offered predictably.

Ken shrugged, knowing that this line of reasoning wouldn't go anywhere; it never did. They'd reached a conversational stalemate. So far as he knew, marijuana had never killed anyone. In fact, the deadliest drugs on the market were cigarettes, alcohol, and prescription painkillers. But, for whatever reason, these got a pass. Someone, somewhere, sometime ago, deemed that these drugs were legal, while these over here were not. There was no rhyme and reason to it. There were only lobbyists and politicians.

So far as Ken was concerned, a person should have the right to put whatever they wanted into their bodies. No one, including the government, should have the power to intervene.

With a sigh, he glanced over his shoulder and made eye contact with one of the guides.

"How much farther to the village?" he asked.

"Ten more," the man answered in a thick Spanish accent.

Ken first looked to the other guide, before remembering that this one didn't speak English at all. He turned to Weathers next.

"Ten more what? Miles? Minutes? Hours?"

Weathers shrugged while the guide went back to hacking through the brush.

"Okay then, I guess—"

Something struck Ken in the shoulder and he stopped midsentence. A round object—some sort of green nut—fell to the ground at his feet and he knelt to pick it up. Tossing it in his palm, Ken wondered what it would be like to live in a place like this, unencumbered by the burdens of a big city. He'd lived his whole life in New York City. In fact, the only time Ken had left the state prior to this trip, was for Operation Eagle Claw in Iran. And that was nothing like *this*. Colombia, for all its faults, was brimming with life. Shit, he was hacking through it right now. Lush, evergreen vegetation, birds constantly—*annoyingly*—chirping. Vibrant music and awful tasting moonshine.

Iran had been different; Iran had been all sand. Sand and *death*.

Ken wasn't disillusioned; New York was far from the safest city in the US, and despite his present experience, Colombia was a dangerous, violent place. But what he'd seen in Iran…

Death was everywhere there. Most people he knew back in the US went their entire lives without seeing death up close. Sure, most everyone knew someone who'd died, but a lifeless body in a beautiful casket wasn't death. That was passing on or moving to a better place or any of the dozen or so euphemisms that people used to describe the end of life.

Real death was seeing a seven-year-old kid with his head caved. Real death was seeing a man being buried up to his neck and stoned by his fellow villagers just for being gay. Real death was seeing limbs scattered around a destroyed building that was supposed to be a military institution but ended up being just a run-of-the-mill apartment.

Limbs that would never be attributed to an owner.

Ken shook his head and then sucked on the wad of dip tucked into his lip before spitting again.

"Ten," the guide repeated, and Ken just shrugged.

The reality was, it didn't matter what unit of measurement the man was referring to. This was the last village they had to visit, and they were going to complete this mission whether it took ten seconds to get there or ten days.

Ken sighed and tossed the nut back into the jungle.

"Yeah, it's good to see that someone agrees with me," Weathers said. "Ten years from now, most of the drugs in the US will come through Mexico, you mark my words."

Chapter 3

'*TEN MORE*' TURNED OUT TO be miles. And, in the sweltering sun chopping their way through thick brush, it felt more like a hundred. Three times Ken had to take a break to sip on his canteen and catch his breath. And during each of these stops, he found his resolve waning.

What the hell is so goddamn important about this last village? If it was critical to anything at all, they would have built a road to it, wouldn't they?

"You glad you answered my call now, Weathers?" he asked between sips of water.

Weathers grunted. Their playful back and forth about the merits of the war on drugs was inversely correlated with their fatigue it seemed.

Ken casually hacked another sapling, then wiped his brow and turned his eyes upward. Their environment couldn't be more different than it had been in Iran. But in some ways, it was also the same. In the desert, you could pass over a single dune and then immediately be lost. There were no landmarks or structures or anything really that could be used to orient oneself. The jungle was like that, too. While the trees were all different, if you took a step back, they all blended into a single green swash, like paint on a canvas.

Ken knew that one could get lost here as easily as they had in the desert not that long ago.

"Weathers, you ever wonder—"

Another one of those damn nuts struck him on the shoulder, but instead of picking it up this time, Ken simply booted it aside. This was the fourth or fifth time that one had fallen on or near him, but for the life of him, Ken couldn't figure out where they were coming from. Sure, the foliage surrounding them was incredibly varied, but he'd yet to identify a tree that produced these kinds of nuts.

"Goddamn fucking birds," he grumbled before turning back to Weathers who was taking a break of his own. "You ever wonder what would happen if we decided not to have this *war* on drugs? If, instead, we decided to regulate them?"

Weathers shook his head as he drank from his canteen. Ken wasn't sure if this gesture was supposed to mean that the man had never thought about it, or if he didn't know what would happen. In the end, it didn't matter; Ken continued with barely a pause.

"Think about it; how many millions or billions of dollars are spent on fighting this war that never ends?"

Another shrug and Ken pressed on.

"Let's just ballpark it as a hundred million dollars, sound fair? All right, so instead of using a hundred million dollars to fight drugs, we use it to educate people on their effects, their dangers. We also put some of that money into drug rehab programs; real programs that help people with their addictions. How would that work?"

"It won't," Weathers said bluntly.

Ken chuckled; the man was nothing if not obstinate.

"You know, I look at the war on drugs akin to taking Tylenol for a brain tumor."

He had Weathers' full attention now.

"Think about it; right now, all we're doing is treating symptoms. In this case, the symptoms are drugs coming into the country. With every other disease, we tackle—or at least try to tackle—the root cause. Sure, we offer symptomatic relief along the way, but the main goal is to treat the cause. We might give Tylenol to someone suffering from a brain tumor, but we don't just wipe our hands clean after that; we use chemo, radiation, surgery. We treat the tumor. But what we don't do, is treat *addiction*."

"Yeah, but that's because chemo cures brain tumors—at least some of them."

The comment piqued Ken's interest and he packed another lip full of chewing tobacco before addressing it.

"So, you're saying that... what? Addiction is palliative? That we can't do anything but—"

Another nut hit him on the shoulder and Ken whipped around.

"Jesus," he swore.

His initial instinct was to look upward, to see if a pesky bird had dropped it on him, but, based on the angle it had fallen, Ken realized that this couldn't be the case. The nut hadn't hit him from above but from the *side*.

His eyes quickly darted to the thick brush to his right and he caught a glimpse of some of the leaves swaying as if someone had just disturbed them. Ken stared for a moment longer, his hand subconsciously tightening on the butt of the rifle strapped across his chest.

Subtle or not, these actions weren't lost on Weathers. The man might be disillusioned and misinformed when it came to the war on drugs, but he was a damn good soldier.

"What is it? What do you see?" Weathers asked flatly.

Ken didn't answer; instead, he raised a fist, indicating for the scientists who were following him to remain still. Up ahead, the guides continued to make a path for them, but Ken ignored them.

He was focused now, homing in on the thick shrubbery to his right.

Did I really see something? Or is it just the heat, exhaustion setting—

"There," he whispered, aiming a finger at a dark figure pressed between two trees. "Weathers? You see that? You see—"

The figure turned and then started to move.

Ken didn't hesitate; he immediately broke into a run.

"Come on, Weathers, try to keep up," he hollered over his shoulder.

Chapter 4

"HE'S THERE!" KEN SHOUTED BETWEEN breaths. Weathers stopped beside him and squinted.

"I don't see him. Anyways, what the fuck does it matter? So, a guy threw a nut at you. It's not the first time that you've been nutted on by a man."

Ken gaped at his friend.

Two jokes in one day? He might actually have heat stroke.

In truth, Ken wasn't sure why he was so driven to find the kid who had thrown the nuts at him.

Perhaps it was all the warnings about drug lords in this part of the country or perhaps it was the sheer audacity of someone throwing something at men strapped with assault rifles.

Or maybe it was simpler than that; maybe he'd just become bored of the jungle and needed some action. Whatever it was, Ken had a hard time letting go.

There was another flash of movement, and then it was gone. A few seconds later, the trees stopped swaying, giving no indication that there had been anybody there in the first place.

Ken shook his head.

"Ah, fuck it. Let's just keep going, get this shit over with. I think the heat is messing with my brain."

Ken turned around and was surprised to see the two guides standing directly behind them, their hands gripping their machetes tightly, eyes wide.

"This way," the one who spoke English said. "You go this way."

Ken shot a glance at Weathers but then shrugged.

"Okay, we go this way," he agreed. He had only taken two steps when Weathers cried out.

He was rubbing the back of his head, a nut on the ground at his heels.

"Looks like you got nutted on, too," Ken said with a chuckle. Then he paused. "There! I see him!"

He broke into a run, pushing by Weathers as he hurried after the boy. The guides were shouting at him, instructing him to go the other way, but Ken ignored them.

He took five steps through the brush before finding himself in a clearing. The change in scenery was so surprising that Ken actually stumbled. Just as he caught his footing, Weathers bowled into him from behind, knocking him to a knee.

The man hit like a truck, whether he meant to or not.

"Clumsy asshole," Ken grumbled, turning his eyes up to Weathers. "You see the kid?"

Weathers shook his head, but then pointed over Ken's shoulder.

"No, but you're not gonna believe this… I see a church."

"A church?" Ken nearly scoffed.

Not believing that anyone would set up a place of worship this deep in the jungle, Ken turned around, thinking that his friend had just beaten his all-time record of jokes in a single day.

"Well smack my ass and call me Sally," Ken muttered under his breath. There, in a clearing roughly the size of a small parking lot, was a modest structure with a cross on top. "It *is* a church. The real question is, who or what are they worshiping?"

Chapter 5

"WHERE'D HE GO?" KEN ASKED, his eyes scanning the small church and the surrounding clearing. The place seemed deserted but couldn't have been; someone had to have removed the foliage from the area. Instead of the soft vegetation of the jungle floor, Ken's feet stirred up a cloud of fine dust or gravel that coated his slick skin.

Weathers shrugged.

"I don't know, but something doesn't feel right about this, Ken. Something—"

Ken rolled his eyes and took another step forward, ignoring his friend. He was starting to sound like a broken record.

Aside from the jokes, that is. Those were new.

"He couldn't have—"

A hand came down on Ken's shoulder, and he instinctively whipped around, leading with the gun. He lowered it when he saw that it was only one of the guides. But when he recognized the fear in the man's face, he didn't let go of the weapon completely.

"We need to go," the guide asserted, actually trying to tug Ken back towards the foliage from which they'd burst through. "We need to go, now."

Ken shrugged the man's hand off and then looked to the other guide who was barely peeking out from between the trees.

"Yeah, I don't think so. Maybe the scientists want to survey this joint."

Ken stared into the man's eyes as he spoke, trying to see if anything changed in them. He'd seen this expression before.

He'd seen it in the eyes of the dead.

The guide swallowed hard, and he took two steps backward, shaking his head the entire time.

"What's your problem, anyway? It's just a church. You afraid of the church?"

The man shook his head even more violently, whipping it back and forth fast enough for sweat to fly off his damp hair. Then he slowly raised a finger and pointed at the church behind Ken. Ken was annoyed and didn't initially take the bait.

"Not God, not church," the guide whispered. "*El diablo*."

Ken's Spanish was rudimentary at best, but that was one term that he did understand. With a hard swallow of his own, he turned and followed the man's trembling finger.

"This ain't like no church I've ever seen," Weathers said, adjusting his gun so that it was aimed out in front of him now.

And yet, Ken still didn't see anything out of the ordinary.

"What? What's going on?"

"There," Weathers said, pointing toward the other side of the clearing. "You see that spike in the ground? Looks like a sapling, but it's coming out of the gravel?"

Ken's eyes finally fell on the item that had struck fear into the guide, and he felt his heart start to race.

"Stay back there, stay with the scientists," Ken instructed the guides, his voice deadpan. "Stay out of sight until I call for you."

Weathers wasn't pointing at the spike, *per se*, but what was mounted on top of it.

Jammed on the sharpened end was a decapitated head. The man's cheeks were blue and purple and swollen, and someone had crudely sewn his lips and eyelids together.

The guide was right. This was the work of *el diablo*.

Chapter 6

CPL. KEN SMITH HUNKERED LOW as he moved sideways, crossing one foot over the other so that his shoulders, and thus his rifle, remained trained on the church at all times. Meanwhile, Weathers did the same thing, only in the opposite direction. When there was a ninety-degree angle between them and the church, they started forward, moving slowly, deliberately, carefully.

Even though he was in stealth mode now, in the back of his mind, Ken reminded himself that the person who had thrown the nuts was only a boy.

He'd seen enough dead children in Iran to know that he didn't want to see any more. They weren't here for him; they were here for whoever had set up the grisly medieval welcome.

At first blush, there didn't appear to be anyone inside the church. The walls of the simple structure were mostly made up of bamboo, and Ken could glimpse through several vertical slits in the side. The interior was too dark to make out anything except for movement, of which he detected none.

As he continued to move forward, Ken noticed a sign out front of the church that contained Spanish writing that he couldn't understand. As he passed it, he nodded to Weathers and then brought a finger to his chest and then pointed at the door.

I'm going in.

Weathers nodded.

Ken had taken roughly a half dozen paces before the door to the church suddenly blew open and a man in a white T-shirt barreled out. He was holding a silver pistol out in front of him.

"Hands up!" Ken shouted.

The man turned to look at him, pulling the gun along for the ride. The last thing Ken wanted to do on this mission was to use his weapon, but he had two young boys back in New York; he didn't want to go home in a body bag, either.

Just as he tensed his finger on the trigger, something struck him on the shoulder drawing his attention.

It was another one of those damn nuts.

That's when he spotted the three men wearing bandannas over their noses and mouths, all brandishing silver handguns, burst from the jungle.

Ken didn't want to fire a single round, but now he saw that he had no choice. A split-second after Weathers opened fire, Ken did the same.

As usual during combat scenarios, Ken didn't think; he let his body, his muscle memory, his training take over.

He saw a muzzle flash from the pistol gripped by the man on the left just before his chest spurted red and he stumbled backwards. He was lucky; the other two men didn't even get a shot off before Ken systematically trained his rifle on them and fired in short bursts.

Like the first felled man, their chests also erupted in a geyser of thick red fluid.

Ken quickly strode forward in his half crouch, approaching them to make sure that they were indeed dead and that they wouldn't be rising from the grave with pistols waving.

After confirming that they were dead, he turned to Weathers and was shocked to see that his partner was now bent over awkwardly.

Cognizant of the fact that more thugs could be hiding in the jungle, Ken kept his eyes on the green foliage as he walked sideways over to Weathers.

"You all right?" he asked over his shoulder.

"I took a bullet, but I should be fine," his partner replied.

Ken nodded and continued to strafe, his eyes scanning for movement. Other than the gentle sway of the leaves in a sudden breeze, there was nothing.

"Anyone inside?"

"Not sure," Weathers answered after a sharp inhale. "I took out the bogey that came out the door, and he ain't getting up."

Ken nodded.

"Can you move? Can you walk?"

The man didn't answer; instead, Ken sensed Weathers rise to his feet at his right. He was grunting and breathing heavily, and a strange hissing sound accompanied every breath.

"Where are the scientists?" Weathers asked.

Ken shook his head.

"Don't know," he said, hoping that the guides had huddled them to safety. There was another question on his mind, too: *Where's the kid? Where's the kid who threw the nuts?*

Ken hadn't overlooked the fact that this distraction had alerted him to the thugs coming out of the jungle, which had likely saved his life. But he couldn't think about that now; the first order of business was to clear the church.

He and Weathers were back-to-back now, seamlessly moving toward the church. Ken was facing the shrubbery near the fallen men, while Weathers had his weapon trained on the church door which still hung open.

He could tell that his partner was laboring, and he felt growing concern now that the hissing sound had taken on a wet quality.

It sounded like a punctured lung.

Ken was suddenly back in the desert, looking for the men that they were supposed to rescue, men that weren't there.

It was all just sand… in every direction all I see is sand…

Sgt. Loomis had warned them that they would be alone on this mission, which made Ken wonder how long it had been since they'd left the last village.

And how long it would take to get back there.

Ten… *something.*

"Any movement from inside?" Ken asked, trying to bring his focus in check.

"No; nothing," Weathers replied.

In his periphery, Ken noticed movement off to the right.

"Hold," he whispered, training his weapon on the area.

When the trees swayed, and a figure pushed through, Ken's finger tensed. Then he pulled it off the trigger upon recognizing the RAND scientist.

The man looked terrified and the front of his khakis was moist from where he'd pissed himself. Behind him was a man in a bandanna, pressing a pistol to the back of the scientist's head.

"Put down your gun," the thug demanded in an accent so thick that Ken could barely understand him.

No matter; his intentions were clear.

"They've got a hostage," Ken whispered over his shoulder.

"Put the gun down," the man hissed again.

Ken focused on what he could see of the man's face above the red bandanna.

He had dark eyes that were narrowed to slits. Beads of sweat dotted his creased forehead.

And then there was his hand; the man was gripping his silver pistol so tightly that his knuckles had started to turn white.

It was clear that the thug was terrified, but it was also clear that he was not afraid to kill. And kill he would, Ken knew it.

He could see it in the man's eyes, his face, his posture.

Ken had no choice. There were five other scientists out there somewhere.

He raised the hand holding the gun in the air while at the same time starting to slip the shoulder strap off.

"*Calma*," he said, using one of the few Spanish words he knew. "*Calma*. We don't care what you're doing here. We're only taking a survey; we mean no harm."

He didn't know if the man understood them, but when he glanced down at his three fallen comrades, the creases around his eyes deepened.

At that moment, Ken realized he'd made a mistake. This man wasn't scared; he was *excited*.

Knowing that he might have to sacrifice this one scientist in order to save the others, Ken quickly lowered his gun again.

"Gun up! Gun up! Gun—"

The man cringed as someone else rushed out of the jungle.

Chapter 7

The guide who barely spoke English stepped forward. Before Ken could stop him, before he could really understand what was going on, the man brought his machete down in a long, sweeping arc. At its zenith, the sunlight reflected off the blade, making it look like some sort of holy beacon.

But rarely had something holy done so much damage. The blade cut deep into the thug's shoulder, nearly severing his arm holding the gun. He cried out and the scientist, sensing, but not seeing, a change, pulled free of his grasp.

And Ken squeezed the trigger.

The top half of the thug's head became the same color as his red bandanna. Brain and blood and bone matter splattered the guide's face, sending him stumbling backwards. He dropped the machete and desperately tried to claw the organic matter from his nose and mouth.

This all happened so quickly that Weathers hadn't even turned around yet, which was for the best.

"More movement from inside the church," he said.

"And we got another bogey down over here," Ken shot back.

A moment later, he felt Weathers tense against his back.

"Don't shoot, don't shoot!" he heard someone shout in a Spanish accent.

Ken quickly glanced over his shoulder and saw a well-built, shirtless man step out of the bamboo structure.

The scene was so strange that Ken's eyes lingered for a second longer than they should have. When he turned back, someone else was emerging, this time sprinting hard to the left.

"HOW MANY ARE THERE?" KEN grumbled, leveling his gun again. But before he could line the blur up, it was gone.

He debated just firing at the disturbed area anyway, but then thought better of it; with his luck, he would've probably taken out all the RAND scientists. He also considered running after the figure, but that would leave Weathers exposed. In the end, he didn't have to do anything; less than a minute later, the man reappeared.

Only he wasn't alone this time. In his arms was a thrashing boy of about six or seven years of age, shouting something in Spanish.

It was *déjà vu*; only this time a boy was held hostage instead of a scientist.

Gritting his teeth, Ken tried to focus on the thug, but the boy kept bucking, making it impossible. During one such violent movement, Ken noticed several unnatural bulges from the pockets of the kid's simple drawstring pants.

The nuts… he was the one who threw the nuts.

"Let him go," the Spanish man who had just exited the church shouted from behind him. "Let him go!"

The man gripping the boy by the waist was taller than the one who'd grabbed the scientist, and his bandanna was black instead of red, but his eyes… they had the same eyes.

They were the eyes of a cold-blooded killer.

And Ken wasn't about to make the same mistake twice.

"Let him go!" the Spanish man continued to holler.

"Gun down!" the thug shouted back.

Goddamn it, just keep still, Ken tried to will the boy. Unlike the scientist, the boy was much shorter than his captor. If he could just stop moving for one second, Ken might have been able to take him out.

But the boy was terrified, and Ken didn't blame him. His legs shot out in front of him, and when the thug readjusted his grip on the boy's waist, several nuts spilled from his pockets. Most stayed near their feet, but one of them rolled right up to Ken.

Knowing that this stalemate could only go on for so long, Ken tried to meet the boy's eyes. And then, by some miracle, they did meet, if only for a moment.

"It's now or never," Ken whispered, hoping that when he kicked the nut, the boy would understand what he meant to do.

After connecting with the toe of his boot, the green oblong shape skipped across the gravel. Just when it hit a stone and took a hard right, the boy leaned over to try and grab it.

That's when Ken once again filled the air with the sound of gunfire.

Chapter 8

"STAY THERE!" WEATHERS SHOUTED. *"STAY the fuck there!"*

But it was clear by the sound of feet striking the gravel that the man from the church wasn't going to listen. As if on cue, the boy pulled himself free of the now dead thug and started running towards Ken, himself.

Unsure of whether they had finally taken out all the threats, Ken kept his gun aimed at the bushes. Just before the boy reached him, the second guide stepped into the clearing along with the five other surveyors. One of them caught a glimpse of all the dead bodies, the carnage, and immediately buckled at the waist and started to vomit. The others covered their eyes like schoolchildren.

"That's all of them," the first guide, the one who had nearly chopped red bandanna's arm off, said.

Ken nodded, but he didn't let his guard down.

"Bogey approaching," Weathers barked over his shoulder.

But Ken was fairly certain at this point that the shirtless man who had exited the church wasn't a bogey; he was just a father who was grateful that his kid had been saved.

"Let him get to his son," Ken said.

Weathers grunted an affirmative, and then he dropped to a knee. Clearly, the bullet he'd taken had done more damage than he was letting on.

Ken would tend to him in a moment, but first, he had to be absolutely certain that nobody was going to pop out of the jungle. But before he could scan the entire perimeter of the clearing, the boy reached him. And, instead of running by him, he surprised Ken by leaping into his arms.

Ken fell backward with the awkward embrace, knocking Weathers to the ground in the process.

"Thank you," the boy said as he hugged Ken. "Thank you, thank you, thank you."

Ken nodded as he waited for the boy's father to peel his son off him.

"You're welcome," he said, rising to his feet and dusting his clothes. The boy's father reiterated the thanks, to which Ken grunted.

"Is that all of them?" he asked, indicating the six downed men with a wave of his hand.

The shirtless man glanced at the corpses in succession, spending at least a few seconds on each of them before moving onto the next. He seemed unmoved by the sight of death.

"*Jes*; that is all of them—for now."

With another nod, Ken shifted the shoulder strap so that the gun was aimed at the ground, then he turned to Weathers.

"Hey, you—"

Ken stopped when he saw that his friend hadn't yet risen back to his feet. In fact, at some point during the boy's embrace, Weathers had fallen on his back and was now looking upward at the waning sun. His face had turned an ashen gray, and his breathing was coming in rapid, wet bursts.

"Fuck," Ken swore, immediately dropping to his knees beside his partner.

It took him only a moment to find the wound: A single bullet hole about three inches below his left pectoral. Deep crimson stained his camouflage shirt and Ken first gently probed the entry wound before snaking his hand behind his friend's back.

His heart sank when he didn't find an exit hole.

Weathers inhaled deeply, his large chest inflating. As he did, Ken heard and felt a sizzle from the orifice in his chest. Bubbles had formed on his torn shirt.

His lung was indeed punctured. And, judging from the amount of blood still pumping from the wound, other organs had also been clipped.

Desperate now, Ken looked up at the guides.

"We need medical," he said. The guide with his face covered in blood shook his head. Ken swore, then turned to the shirtless man who was still holding his son tightly. "Please, you need to help us; do you have any medical supplies in the church?"

Chapter 9

KEN GRUNTED AS HE DRAGGED Weathers across the gravel and then up the small steps of the church. The man's lips had started to take on a bluish hue, and his breaths were accompanied by a hiccup now with almost every inhale.

He should have cleared the church first, but Weathers was running out of time. When Ken finally made it inside, what he saw nearly took his breath away. The church wasn't empty, far from it. But it wasn't filled with gang bangers, either.

Inside, were three women, another child, and more heroin than he could ever imagine. The interior of the church itself reeked of vinegar so strongly that Ken's eyes started to water almost immediately. The fumes were strong and likely caustic to a man with a lung injury, but he had to get Weathers out of the sun. Fighting his gag reflex, he yanked Weathers through the doorway.

The women in the church were all huddled to one side, scared, but evidently not dangerous. Ken got the feeling that these people weren't here on their own accord, and that the severed head on the spike was a reminder of what might happen to them if they attempted to leave.

"Hospital," he said. "Please, we need to get this man to a hospital."

The closest woman, apparently not understanding, simply shook her head, but another, this one much older than the rest, strode forward. She began rustling through a pile of papers, before coming up with a bag emblazoned with a red cross on it.

As soon as he saw the small dimensions of the bag, Ken felt whatever fleeting hope he had left eke from his pores. In truth, he didn't know what he was expecting, but whatever it was, it wasn't going to be inside a six-by-eight-inch satchel.

Nothing in there would fix a punctured lung.

Shaking his head, Ken rose to his feet and pulled the satellite phone from his hip. The woman opened the bag and started to tend to Weathers as Ken dialed Sgt. Loomis' number. When he saw that there was no signal, he made his way outside, inhaling deeply.

He managed to snag one bar and then redialed Loomis. The phone rang once, and then a male voice answered. Ken promptly gave his call sign and waited to be transferred.

"Cpl. Smith, this better be an emergency, because—"

"Weathers has been shot," Ken interrupted. With his free hand, he started to massage his temples. He couldn't believe how badly things had turned, and so quickly. In Iran, they'd been expecting this sort of thing, had prepared for it. But not here. Not while doing a stupid goddamn survey.

I should've stayed on the path, I should've stayed behind the guides like they'd said.

"Weathers has been shot, and it's bad. I need immediate evac." Ken pulled the phone away from his ear and read the coordinates from the dot matrix display. "It's gotta be quick."

When Sgt. Loomis didn't immediately respond, Ken confirmed that he still had a signal.

"Did you hear me? Weathers is hurt—bullet in the lung, he's not gonna make it much longer. We need immediate evac."

The man on the other end of the line uttered a heavy sigh, and Ken dreaded what was coming next.

"That's a negative, Cpl. Smith; the closest evac is in Ecuador. You're gonna have to hold tight for the night.

Ken glanced back into the church and saw that even with the woman tending to his wounds, Weathers' body had started to tremble.

The night? He's not going to make it through the hour.

"No... no, not the night. Weathers isn't gonna make it 'til sundown."

"Do your best to make him comfortable, then," Loomis said, his voice flat.

Ken squeezed his temples. He couldn't believe it, he couldn't believe that he'd convinced Weathers to come here.

He couldn't believe that he brought his best friend here to die.

"I can have evac there for you at 0600 hours. Nothing earlier." There was a short pause before Loomis offered, "I'm sorry."

Ken just shook his head. No amount of arguing would change the sergeant's mind at this point.

"Understood," Ken said softly, before signing off. He tucked the phone back onto his belt and then made his way back into the church, Sgt. Loomis' words echoing in his mind.

Make him comfortable.

Ken dropped to his knees and squeezed his partner's hand in his own. Weathers slowly turned his head to look at him, and what he saw in the man's dark eyes brought tears to his own.

It wasn't disdain, nor was it even anger. It was something else.

It was sheer futility. Utter helplessness.

In the reflection of the man's moist eyes, Ken could see the same expression on his own face.

There was nothing at all he could do but make his friend comfortable.

Ken wiped the tears from his cheeks and turned to the elderly woman.

"Can you give him something?"

The woman frowned, and Ken glanced deliberately over at the barrels of heroin.

"Please."

The woman seemed to understand now, and she started to rise.

Ken turned his attention back to Weathers and squeezed the man's large hand tightly.

"I'm sorry," he whispered. "I'm sorry, man. There's nothing… fuck, there's nothing I can do."

Chapter 10

KEN SMITH PACKED CHEWING TOBACCO into his lip and stared out into the brush, his hand resting comfortably on the butt of his rifle.

He'd been standing this way for pretty much the entire night. And now that he could sense the sun struggling to rise, to shed illumination on the dense foliage before him, Ken finally felt the familiar tug of fatigue.

This wasn't the first time that he'd gone an entire night without sleep. Back in Iran, he'd survived for nearly three whole days hopped up on chewing tobacco and coffee grinds. But this was different. In Iran, his best friend's corpse wasn't lying a couple dozen feet away.

He'd cried on and off throughout the night. The feeling of knowing that his friend was gasping for breath and there was nothing he could do was indescribable.

At least he hadn't suffered; the old ladies in the church had seen to that.

The guides had long since left, taking the RAND Scientists to their final village to complete the mission.

Ken had watched them go.

He had to stay with Weathers; it was the least he could do. Every once in a while, one of the members of the church, three generations of the same family who had been held captive, would bring him a cup of water.

He was grateful.

They'd also brought him food, but he'd declined.

Someone cleared their throat, and Ken turned, surprised to find the man from the church at his side.

"That was my father," the man said in a thick accent. He raised a finger and pointed at the outline of the head on the spike. "We went as a family to visit a local farm one day; on the way home, a van pulled in front of our car and blocked our path. The door opened and men with guns got out. My father resisted, but they beat him severely. Before we knew what was happening, they threw us all in the van, brought us out here. That was more than three years ago."

Ken could barely believe his ears.

"Three years?"

The man nodded.

"They kept telling us that all we had to do is make one more batch and then they would take us home. But after about six months, it became obvious that this wasn't the case. My father tried to break away, promising to get us help. But they caught him; they caught him and did *that*. After, we didn't think about running anymore. We just accepted that this is our life from now on."

Ken looked at the man, unsure of what was more shocking, the fact that they had been kidnapped over three years ago, or that he spoke so candidly about his father's murder and decapitation.

"We just accepted it," the man repeated, turning his eyes to the horizon.

Ken spat brown tobacco juice on the gravel at his feet.

"Well, you're free to go now," he said absently.

The man at his right didn't say anything for some time. Eventually, Ken looked over at him again, if for nothing else but to make sure he was still there.

He was.

"Where would we go?" the man asked. "We've been gone for three years. Our family and friends think that we're dead. Our house has been sold, our jobs given to others. We go back, and we have nothing. We go back, and we are as helpless as we were here before you came."

Ken thought about this for a moment. He thought about how horrible it must be to be taken from your home, to be transplanted here in the jungle with only the clothes on your back and instructions on how to manufacture heroin and cocaine and whatever else they might have cooked inside the tiny church.

How helpless one must feel.

Ken turned to look at the sign that marked the entrance to the church, the one with the Spanish text and the strange symbol of a snake devouring an eyeball on it.

"*Iglesia de Liberacion,*" the man said, following his gaze.

Ken raised an eyebrow and the man translated.

"The Church of Liberation."

Ken couldn't help but think of how the man and his family felt staring at that sign for three full years.

"They'll be back, you know," the man said, his eyes returning to the horizon. "Where there are drugs, there's power. And that draws the bad people."

"And what are you going to do?" Ken asked absently.

The man moved his hand to the gun tucked into his belt, which he'd pried away from one of the dead thugs.

"What I have to," he said after a deep breath. "The question is, what are you going to do?"

Chapter 11

FOR THE FIRST TIME IN as long as he could remember, Ken Smith wasn't sure *what* he was going to do. He was grieving, of that he was certain, as was the fact that he was going back to New York.

Without his best friend, that is.

He figured that Sgt. Loomis would give him some time off and then likely set him up with some cushy local gig.

But what of Carl Weathers? He was destined to become a faceless tragedy that would quickly be pushed under the rug by the US military and the RAND Corporation. Sure, Ken *could* go to the press, tell them what had really happened here, that Weathers died protecting a half dozen scientists, but what would that serve?

People wouldn't look at Carl as a hero, but with scorn. A black smear on the U.S. Army, on peacekeeping efforts in general.

On the ridiculous War on Drugs.

And then what? In a week, Weathers would be forgotten again, and Ken would be without a job. Nobody liked a whistleblower, a troublemaker.

Nobody.

Ken's eyes drifted from the horizon back to the interior of the church. The door was wide open, and he could see the little boy he'd saved sleeping on a cot surrounded by what was likely a few million dollars' worth of heroin.

Weathers died for this? For a fucking powder? A powder, a commodity, that people wanted?

Ken shook his head.

It made no sense.

None of it made any sense.

"When they come back, I'll be ready," the man at his right said.

Ken turned his attention to the shirtless man. It was clear that he too was damaged. After all, his father had been murdered and his decapitated head placed on a spike as a warning to him and his family.

But this man was not a pushover. He'd done what he had to do to protect his family—the rest of his family. But now that he had weapons at his disposal, Ken suspected that he would take a proactive approach.

That he would grab his newfound power and wield it.

An idea suddenly occurred to Ken. Sure, he could go back to New York, fall in line like a good little soldier.

His eyes fell on the sign with the snake eating the eyeball and the words *Iglesia de Liberacion* written across the top.

Or he could do something else… he could turn Weathers' death from a tragedy into something positive. He could spin it, make him a hero for liberating the three generations of captives.

Ken reached up and pinched the bridge of his nose. He was exhausted, more so even than those days when he'd gone seventy-two hours without sleep.

He wasn't sure what to do.

But he knew what he *didn't* want to do. He didn't want to be taken advantage of. He no longer wanted to be the hired hand; he wanted to be the person who hired others to do his bidding for him.

Never again did Ken want to feel as helpless as he had today.

"We can work together," the man said suddenly.

Ken once again looked at the impish man with a deeply tanned skin and the bristly mustache.

Work together?

"I know a way to get the product into the US. I know *things*."

He whistled shrilly, and, in his periphery, Ken saw the boy in the church rise from his slumber. He looked at his father, nodded, and then hurried out of view.

A few seconds later, the boy returned with two packages in his hands. They were wrapped in brown paper and taped together using red tape with the snake eating the eyeball symbol on it.

"Take them," the man said. Ken just stared at the packages for a moment. "It's a reward for saving him. For saving us."

Ken's initial instinct was to decline the offer, to shake his head and say, *No thanks.*

But why shouldn't he take them? Why shouldn't he take them back to New York and give the money to Weathers' family? The man had children, for Christ's sake. Just one of these packages would be enough to put his daughters through college when the time came.

Ken glanced back into the church.

Imagine what I could do with more?

Ken then looked at himself and sighed.

Even if he had the gall to smuggle the drugs, where would he put them? It's not like you could hide a few kilos of heroin in your pockets and nobody would notice.

He started to shake his head when the man suddenly grabbed his arm.

"The helicopter is coming," he said. "And I think they bring a box for your friend?"

A box for my friend? What the—

And then he realized what the man was saying.

They would indeed bring a box—a coffin—to transport Weathers' body first back to Bogotá, before being flown to the United States. And Ken would be with that box at all times.

Ken smirked.

Yeah, this man had it all figured out. He may have been held captive for three years, but he had clearly put some thought into what would happen if the tables were ever turned.

Ken scooped the tobacco out of his mouth with his finger and flung it to the dirt.

Why shouldn't he be the one to import the drugs? They were going to get into the country with or without him.

The sound of helicopter blades chuffing finally reached Ken's ears. It was time to shoot a flare, let Loomis or whoever the man had sent know exactly where he was.

Which meant that it was also time to make a decision.

Without thinking, Ken pulled a camera out of his pocket and handed it to the young boy who set down the bricks before accepting it. He looked to his father, who said something quickly in Spanish, to which the boy nodded.

Turn this from a tragedy into something positive.

Ken and the man walked over to the sign for the Church of Liberation and stood in front of it. With a deep breath, Ken put his arm around the man's shoulder and motioned for the boy to raise the camera. When the kid started counting down in Spanish from three, Ken surprised himself by managing a fairly genuine-looking smile.

As the helicopter neared and Ken set off the flare, the man approached him again and stared him directly in the eyes.

"Ken Smith, you saved my son—I am grateful for what you did."

Ken nodded and shook the man's hand.

"I think… I think maybe we *should* work together," he continued. "I think we could do very good things, make a lot of money."

Ken tried to pull his hand away, but the man held fast. He was surprised by how much strength the stocky man possessed.

With a curt nod, the man finally released him.

"I never even got your name," Ken said in a soft voice.

It was difficult to hear himself think over the sound of the approaching helicopter, but for some reason, Ken heard the words from the man's mouth loud and clear.

It was as if he knew him already.

"My name is Raul; Raul Mendes. When you're ready, come back for me, Ken Smith. When you're ready, we will do great business together."

PART II

The Jungle

PRESENT DAY

Chapter 12

"WAKE UP. WAKE UP, *GRINGO*."

Damien Drake groaned and opened his eyes. His head was foggy, his muscles ached, and there was a foul taste in his mouth.

"Are we there?" he grumbled into the darkness.

"No, we ain't there yet. Pit stop. Y'all got one hour. Do whatever you want, but don't miss the boat. We leave in one hour," the captain's familiar voice informed him.

With a great effort, Drake managed to pull himself into a seated position. The cot in which he slept was about as comfortable as a sheet of nails, which contributed to his general soreness instead of alleviating it.

But beggars couldn't be choosers.

A flickering light bulb suddenly illuminated the darkness, and Drake shielded his eyes. He could sense others rising from their slumber around him, muttering in Spanish and grunting and groaning much as he had moments ago.

After a series of tentative blinks, he became accustomed to the lighting and reached into his bag for a fresh pair of underwear. It was the last clean item of clothing that he had. He slipped them on, then got dressed in his jeans and T-shirt. Both smelled of sweat, but that was par for the course below deck.

Following a quick, and ineffective stretch, Drake slipped his trusty bag over one shoulder and looked around.

The Colombians were all busy packing up their things as well, all focused on their own paltry set of belongings. All but one, that is; the man, who had called him *el phantasmo* the night before and shared his horrible liquor, was looking right at him.

They'd spoken quite a bit last night, but Drake could only remember bits and pieces. Something about how the man had to flee the country after a drug deal gone bad. Something about having to leave to protect his family.

What Drake couldn't remember for the life of him, was why the man was going back.

After their mutual stare bordered on uncomfortable, Drake nodded, and the man looked away.

Forcing his stiff legs into action, Drake slowly made his way topside.

And what he saw took his breath away.

Based on the condition of the fishing vessel and its occupants, he'd suspected that their pit stop would take place at some toothless hillbilly's rotting dock.

This couldn't have been further from reality.

The captain had pulled up to an island cut straight out of a travel magazine. The water surrounding them was a crystal blue, the sky a pleasant tangerine as the sun awoke with the rest of them, and the foliage lush and verdant.

Drake was so taken aback by this unexpected beauty that even though his intentions had been to use a real toilet for once and maybe score something to eat, he did neither; instead, he simply stood on the deck, his hands clenching the rusted metal railing.

"You can stay here if you want," a gruff voice from behind him stated. Drake looked over at the captain, who somehow looked worse than the stowaways below deck. "You could just stay here."

Drake stared at the man for a moment before turning his attention back to the island.

This wasn't his destination, and he knew better than to be wooed by shiny objects. He had one mission, one objective: to find Ken Smith and make the man pay for the lives he'd ruined in his insatiable quest for power.

But that didn't mean he had to suffer intentionally along the way. After all, he wasn't some sort of sadist, was he?

Instead of answering, Drake patted the man on the shoulder and then started towards the dock.

When the captain hollered after him, his tone had changed; no longer was it sympathetic, caring.

It was harsh, the way the voice of a captain should be.

"One hour. If you ain't back in one hour, yous gonna stay here."

Drake nodded.

It could be worse, he supposed. There were definitely worse places to be stranded on this earth than this beautiful island.

Chapter 13

"CLOSE YOUR EYES; SERIOUSLY, LEROY, Hanna, close your damn eyes," Screech said as he placed a hand on the small of each of their backs and gently guided them forward.

"I swear to God, if this is some sort of weird sex game..."

Screech shoved Hanna forward a little more forcefully.

"Just play along, I swear you'll like it."

"Hmmm, that's what my last boyfriend said, and he ended up in the 'merge,'" Hanna grumbled.

Screech ignored her.

"All right, all right, slow... slow... okay, stop."

"Can I open my eyes now?" Leroy asked.

"No, not yet." Screech quickly moved in front of the duo, making sure that his body was blocking their view of the door behind him. "Now, open your eyes."

He was beaming, and he expected this expression to be reflected on Hanna's and Leroy's faces.

He was disappointed.

Leroy had something akin to a sneer on his lips while Hanna looked about as pleased as someone finding porcupine quills in their tomato soup.

"What the hell is this? Some sort of barbershop?" Hanna asked.

Screech looked skyward.

"A barbershop? No... no, it's..."

Instead of finishing the sentence, Screech stepped to one side and waved a hand dramatically in front of the frosted door.

"Oh! I know! An eye exam clinic!" Leroy chimed in. "It's an eye exam clinic."

Screech scowled.

"No, it's not a fucking optometrist's office or barbershop or abortion clinic. It's our new headquarters."

Leroy raised an eyebrow and Hanna chewed her bottom lip. The latter leaned in close to the lettering on the door, and then suddenly pulled back, eyes wide.

"Is that… is that…"

Screech's smile returned, and he nodded, turning his attention to the fancy decal that he'd stuck to the door just a few hours ago.

"Yep, it's—"

"You were right, Leroy," Hanna continued. "It *is* some sort of eye test."

Screech threw up his hands.

"For fuck's sake guys, this isn't an eye test; they're our initials and this is our new office," he moved a finger across the decal as he spoke. "DSLH Investigations."

Leroy suddenly burst out laughing and clapped him on the back.

"We're just fucking with you, Screech. It looks amazing."

Screech looked at Leroy, trying to figure out if he was being serious. Then he glanced over at Hanna who was smiling now. She ran a hand through her dark hair, which had since grown in.

"Well, aside from the fact that my name is last, and that Drake gets his last name on the door and we get our first names…" She let the sentence trail off before suddenly embracing Screech in a tight hug. "Just kiddin'. Leroy's right; it looks amazing."

After disengaging from Hanna, Screech took a step back to inspect his handiwork.

It wasn't just a new door, of course, it was a new office, as well.

But it was also more than that. It was a new beginning.

Drake should be here with us, he thought unexpectedly. *After all, you started all this. Without you, I —*

Hanna, clearly sensing that the mood was about to change, reached past Screech and grabbed the door handle.

"Come on, show us the inside. I can't wait to see my corner office and meet my sexy secretary," she said with a grin.

Chapter 14

THE ISLAND, WHICH DRAKE HAD since discovered was the Virgin Gorda, wasn't exactly what he'd expected. He was hoping for some basic amenities, like a coffee shop or somewhere he could grab a bite to eat and maybe restock for the last leg of the journey to Colombia. But it appeared that they'd docked on some sort of private resort, which only added to the confusion. How the foul-smelling captain had arranged this locale for refueling was a mystery that might never be solved.

Drake ended up walking around several villas before finally coming upon what appeared to be a main reception hall of sorts.

The good news was that it appeared to be the off-season and the place was almost deserted. He wasn't one for designer clothes and fancy watches during the best of times, but boy did he stink right now.

Still, he had more important things to expend mental energy on.

Drake walked slowly to the front desk, trying his best not to look like either a vagrant or a potential armed robber. Halfway across the lavish foyer, however, he changed his mind. Sneaking up on the man behind the desk who was hammering away at his keyboard likely wasn't a good idea, either.

To announce his presence, he cleared his throat and the maître d' raised his eyes from his computer. They went wide for a moment, then he actually stumbled backward.

"*El phantasmo,*" the man breathed.

Drake showed the man his palms.

"No, I'm sorry, didn't mean to startle you. I just wondered if there was somewhere around here that I could get a cup of coffee. I have money."

The man blinked several times, and then took a deep breath and collected himself.

"No, *I'm* sorry. I thought you were someone else. Are you with the… with the fishing vessel? Just stopping in for a short while?" the man asked, raising an eyebrow. He was young, dressed in a perfectly tailored suit, and his dark hair was coiffed to one side.

"Just an hour," Drake replied hesitantly.

At least he knows about the fishing vessel.

"Can I get a coffee? Maybe a shower?"

The man stared at him for a moment too long.

"Look, I—"

The man smiled uncomfortably.

"No, I'm sorry. It's just… well, never mind. Would you like to freshen up in the same villa that your friend had?"

Confusion washed over Drake and he rubbed his eyes, wishing that he hadn't drunk so much of the horrible swill that the man on the boat had handed him.

"I'm sorry? My friend?"

Drake took a deep breath and then looked around, thinking that the entire time the man might have been speaking to someone else, that he really was just *el phantasmo*.

But he was the only one here.

"The man with the blond hair and the tattoos? He's not your friend?"

Once again, Drake shook his head.

"I don't know who—wait, blond guy, you said? Kinda annoying, likes to make inappropriate jokes?"

The maître d's smile widened.

"Yes, yes, Dr. Campbell. He was here not too long ago. He helped us—" the man's smile faltered, "Well, he helped us take care of some unruly guests."

Drake's brow furrowed.

"Yeah, I know Beckett. But how did you… shit, what did he do, exactly?"

The maître d' waved a hand dismissively.

"Oh, nothing—nothing, really. But any friend of Beckett is a friend of ours. I will let you freshen up in one of the villas. And if you want to stay…"

Drake started to shake his head and the man nodded curtly.

"Sure, I get it. You're on a voyage. But if at any point you want to return, you will be well taken care of."

"Uh, thanks," Drake said hesitantly. This entire interaction had him confused and bewildered.

The maître d' reached below the counter and then handed Drake a set of keys.

"Oh, and not to worry, the sheets have been changed since your friend's visit."

"Amen to that," Drake said with a grimace. "Amen to that."

Chapter 15

"HOLY SHIT," LEROY GASPED, "*THIS* is triple D investigations?"

Screech shook his head.

"No, this is DSLH Investigations," he corrected.

Leroy didn't appear to hear him. Instead, he simply looked about the room as if stepping onto a strange planet.

"Kinda stupid name," Hanna grumbled, and Screech smiled; he couldn't agree more. But at least it didn't sound like a strip club—Triple D Investigations. "Where's the boss man's desk?"

Screech turned his attention to the four desks arranged in a half circle towards the back of the room.

"There are no offices. This is an… what do you call it? An open concept style space. We've got a desk at the front for a secretary—which, before you say it, we don't have yet—then we have seating space for clients—which we also don't have yet—and the other desks are for us. It's supposed to invoke trust with our future clients."

Hanna looked over at him.

"Where'd you read that, Cosmo?"

"Teen Beat," Screech shot back.

"Well, what about more, uh, sensitive matters? Also, where can we drink and fuck?" Hanna asked.

Screech looked away, his cheeks turning red.

"There's a broom closet for that," he grumbled.

"So, which one's mine?" Leroy nearly shouted, his excitement lifting the entire attitude of the room.

Screech shrugged.

"Whichever one you want."

Leroy didn't hesitate; he ran to the glass desk on the far right. Then he plopped himself down in the chair, spun around once, and then embraced his computer monitor.

"This is… *amazing.*"

Screech chuckled.

He was proud of where they'd come from, even given the tumultuous route they'd taken.

"Yeah, it is amazing. *Too* amazing. How can we afford all this?" Hanna asked.

Screech had expected some incredulity, but cynicism had been Drake's department, not Hanna's. He smiled meekly.

"Let's just say that Triple D made some shrewd investments along the way. I will emphasize, though, that if we want to keep this space, we're gonna need to acquire some clients, ASAP."

"I'll do anything so long as we don't have to go back to the shithole we came from," Leroy admitted.

"Touché," Hanna said, as she made her way over to one of the other desks and took a seat.

Screech selected his desk but couldn't help looking over at the last one.

The empty one.

The one that belonged to Drake.

He sighed.

"Your computer login is your name, the password is our initials, just like on the door," Screech informed the others.

They all spent the better part of ten minutes mucking about on their computers before boredom eventually set in.

"Well? What the hell do we do now?" Hanna asked.

Screech made a face. He'd done a lot for Triple D and he'd been there since the very beginning. And while he'd gone way above and beyond just computer duties, one thing he hadn't participated in was client recruitment. They just sort of... fell into their lap.

Or, more accurately, into *Drake's* lap.

"Well?"

Screech shrugged.

"Now we just wait for—" There was a sudden knock on the door and Screech leaned backward in surprise. The tightly coiled springs in his brand-new chair flung him back upright so quickly that he nearly knocked the monitor off his desk. "— a client," he said softly.

Chapter 16

THERE WAS A STRANGE SMELL to the room. Not a particularly *bad* smell, but a bitterness that was difficult to describe. What made it worse, however, was that Drake couldn't tell exactly where it was coming from. As the maître d' had promised, the sheets were clean, and the rest of the villa was pristine.

And yet that smell…

Drake's eyes lingered on the expertly made bed, and he wondered if one day he might be able to take the maître d' up on his offer, if it indeed was a serious one.

If one day he would be able to just lay his head down and rest, for once.

Without dreams.

He shook his head and then slowly made his way to the shower and turned on the hot water, deliberately avoiding his reflection in the mirror. When the water temp hit scalding, he stripped down and stepped inside.

Even though he hadn't glanced in the mirror, as he washed the grime from his body, Drake couldn't help but notice the wounds that peppered his flesh.

There was a dark blue stain across his right side as if his liver was desperately trying to force its way through his translucent skin. There was his injured shoulder, the scar from the bullet in his calf. Drake even pushed his tongue into the space in his lower gum where his tooth had once taken up residence.

Yeah, I really could sleep for a year.

After he'd finished washing off a layer of dirt, and maybe even a layer of skin, Drake dried himself off and slipped back into his clean underwear. He debated going to the front desk and asking if he could have his clothes washed but thought better of it.

The captain had given him an hour, and he didn't doubt that he would push off with or without Drake. As he left the villa, he took one final look back, and pictured Beckett staying here.

Beckett, who had helped the maître d' deal with some unruly guests.

They'd been friends for nearly a decade, and Drake had thought that he knew the man well, better than most, perhaps. But recently, ever since Craig Sloan, the man had changed. He was—

Drake shook his head to clear his thoughts and closed the door behind him.

He hurried back to the reception hall and tossed the keys to the maître d'.

"Mr. Drake, I hope you've enjoyed the facilities," the man said with a smile.

"I did, thank you," Drake grumbled. He was about to turn and leave, when a thought occurred to him.

"Is there something else I can help you with?"

Drake rooted through his bag and eventually pulled out a worn photograph.

"Maybe," he said, passing the photo over to the man. "When's the last time you saw this boat?"

The maître d's eyes flicked down to the black and white image of *B-Yacht'ch* and his smile faltered. But when he looked back up at Drake, his face looked exactly as it had before: pleasant and welcoming.

"The last time I saw this yacht, your friend the doctor was on it. He was heading back to New York, I believe."

Drake wasn't the best at telling when people were lying —
case in point Jasmine's deception — but he was getting better at
it.

And when the maître d's pupils dilated, and his hand had a
slight tremor to it when he handed the photo back, Drake
knew that this man wasn't telling the truth.

"Hmm," Drake said, pressing his lips together tightly. He
was about to add more when he heard the sound of a horn
blaring in the distance.

"Mr. Drake, I'm afraid that your ship is leaving soon."

Drake jammed the photograph back into his pocket.

"Yeah, I think my time here is up," he said, turning toward
the door. "Thanks for the shower."

"Oh, you're very welcome, Drake. And I really do hope
that I see you again someday. Perhaps on your return voyage,
you would be interested in staying longer and really taking
advantage of the wonderful amenities we have here at the
Virgin Gorda?"

"Yeah, maybe…"

…if there is a return voyage.

Chapter 17

"ANNNNND OUR FIRST CLIENT IS A non-paying one," Hanna muttered under her breath.

Screech shook his head and opened the door wide. The man who barged into DSLH looked older than he remembered, and his demeanor was off. After what they'd done, after putting Raul in handcuffs and Ken Smith fleeing and the subsequent fallout, he expected him to be cheery, happy, grateful, even.

Instead, the man looked miserable.

"Gee, come on in, Sgt. Yasiv," Screech said, closing the door behind the man.

Yasiv's eyes were low when he entered, but when he found himself bathed in bright, incandescent lighting, he raised his head, the expression on his face transitioned from dejected to confused. When he noticed Leroy and Hanna staring at him, his confusion only grew.

"Nice place you got here," he said at last. His voice had rough edges to it, as if he were suffering from laryngitis.

"Thanks," Screech replied with a nod. "To what do we owe the honor?"

Yasiv looked around nervously, his eyes deliberately falling first on Hanna, then Leroy.

"Is there somewhere private we can talk?"

Now it was Screech's turn to glance around. His first instinct was to recommend the broom closet—it was actually a small office, but Hanna didn't need to know that—but eventually, he found himself shaking his head. Drake may have had his secret wheeling and dealings at Triple D, but Drake wasn't around, and this wasn't Triple D.

It was Screech's capital that funded the place, and they were all equal partners now.

"Whatever you want to say to me, you can say in front of Leroy and Hanna."

His authoritative tone surprised even himself, but he also felt a tinge of pride deep down in his gut. Screech wasn't sure how long Drake was going to be away, and he'd be the first one to admit that he had reservations about taking the helm. Equal partners or not, somebody had to steer the ship, and given his experience—paltry as it was—that responsibility fell squarely on his shoulders.

And this seemed like a positive step for him—for all of them.

Yasiv frowned.

"Okay, okay—if you want it that way, fine. I've come here to discuss two things. The first is Drake."

Just mentioning the man's name seemed to suck the air out of the room.

"What about him?" Screech asked, eyes narrowing. "Like I told the goon squad when they questioned me, I don't know where he went after the incident at Ken Smith's condo. I don't—"

Yasiv shook his head.

"Yeah, I know, I know. It's not about where he is now, it's about what's going to happen when he comes back."

"What do you mean?"

The air returned into the room, only now it was thick with tension.

Yasiv looked down.

"I'm doing the best I can here, I just want you to know that. Drake's a friend to me."

Screech felt his temperature start to rise.

"What are you talking about?" he demanded.

Yasiv's eyes snapped up.

"I'm talking about keeping him out of jail. I'm doing the best I can."

"What? What do you mean you're 'doing the best you can?' Drake was the one who brought in the evidence that forced Ken to abandon his post as mayor and flee the city. He's the one who helped you get the indictments against Raul and Palmer and all those other high-ranking police officers the talking heads on the news are always jibber-jabbering about. And yet he's still facing jail time?"

Sgt. Yasiv pulled a cigarette from the pack in his pocket and brought it to his lips. Before he could light up, however, Screech stepped forward.

"There's no smoking in here," he snapped. His face had gotten hot, and Screech could feel his temper getting away from him.

He's a friend, Screech reminded himself. *He's also a good person to have on your side. Keep it together.*

"Sorry," Yasiv grumbled, tucking the smoke behind his ear. "It's just his fucking luck."

Screech's upper lip curled.

"What's just his luck? Drake got those men, Yasiv. He should be a hero, he should—"

"Hero might be a stretch, but he is a good man, Screech, I'll give you that. There were one-hundred and twenty-two indictments passed down due to Ken Smith's fallout, but guess who just happened to be squeaky clean? Guess who wasn't included in those indictments?"

"Kramer," Screech replied instinctively.

Yasiv nodded.

"Yeah, Officer Kramer. I've done everything to try to convince him and the DA to lessen the charges, or even drop them entirely, but, man, Kramer is still so sour about what happened to Cuthbert. He won't budge. Stubborn as a fucking mule, that guy."

Screech was incredulous.

"You can't be serious; it wasn't even Drake who hit the guy. It was..." Screech let his sentence trail off. There was no point throwing Mandy under the bus and, besides, given what he knew about Kramer and Drake's relationship, he doubted the truth would make any difference.

"I know, I know," Yasiv said softly. "But that doesn't change the fact that he threw Kramer into a fucking shipping container. Like I said, I'm still trying to work Kramer, but right now the best I can do is to pressure the DA for the shortest jail time. Just a—"

Screech suddenly lost the battle with his temper.

"Jail time? *Jail time?* Drake's gonna get jail time? You can't be serious. He'll be killed in there."

Yasiv sighed but offered nothing in terms of a response.

"What a fucking joke," Hanna said, speaking up for the first time.

Yasiv suddenly leveled his eyes at the woman, anger creeping onto his features.

"I'm doing the best I fucking can. Don't forget that I managed to keep your ass out of prison for helping that psychopath Marcus Slasinsky escape, which, by the way, the only reason isn't bigger news is because of what happened with the mayor. Don't forget *that.*"

Hanna looked like she was about to say something, shoot back a snide remark, perhaps, but for once she managed to keep her mouth shut.

Screech took a deep breath and his anger started to recede.

"Okay, okay. We're all friends here. Just keep working on Kramer, do whatever you can to get him to drop the charges."

"That's what I'm doing. But the man still blames Drake for what happened to Clay Cuthbert. Even after everything that's happened, he still blames Drake."

Screech cocked his head to one side as he thought about this for a moment. A few years back, he might have thought this ridiculous, that there was just something wrong with Kramer. But his recent exposure to death had taught him a few things about how survivors dealt with the guilt of remaining behind.

Kramer was still hurting, and he wanted someone to pay for his pain. He couldn't parlay these emotions onto the real people responsible—like the Church of Liberation, Ray Reynolds, or Ken Smith—because they were either dead or missing; they were ghosts. The man needed his pain and anger to be rooted in a real person, someone who still had something to lose.

And that person was Damien Drake.

Screech's eyes drifted to his desk drawer where he'd put a bottle of Johnny Blue for Drake when—or if—the man returned. The gesture had been meant as a joke, a throwback reminder of where they used to work, but he was surprised to realize that it was now calling his name.

He shook his head.

"Okay, okay... you said you came here for *two* reasons. Please tell me that you started with the bad news. I don't know how much more of this shit I can take."

Chapter 18

THE NEXT TIME DRAKE AWOKE, the fishing vessel had just touched down. Only they hadn't landed in a busy port as he expected, but some sort of dilapidated dock that was nestled away from prying eyes.

I should have expected as much, he thought as he made his way topside.

When he saw the extent of the vegetation—the portion of the dock attached to land was so overgrown that it was nearly impassable without a cutlass—Drake could only shake his head.

His hope was to get started on foot immediately, start his search for Ken, but, clearly, he hadn't thought this through.

What else is new?

He held out hope that this was just another pit stop, but when he spotted the captain tying up the vessel while chain-smoking cigarettes, he knew that this wasn't the case.

"One-way ticket," the man said when their eyes met, confirming Drake's suspicion.

Drake nodded and watched as the Colombians quickly and silently dispersed into the jungle. They disappeared so quickly that he wondered for a moment if they weren't the *el phantasmo* and not him.

With a heavy sigh, he stared at the jungle before him.

As usual, he hadn't thought through the finer points of the plan; only big, grandiose ideas for Damien Drake.

Find Ken and find out what happened to Dane, he reminded himself. *In and out. That's it.*

"Fuck," Drake grumbled as he stepped onto the dock.

"I'm heading back to the island to refuel," the captain said absently as he lit another cigarette with the butt of the first. It was a simple, ambiguous statement, but the man's meaning was clear.

Despite the captain's claim that the ten grand was for a one-way voyage, if he wanted to, Drake could join him for some R and R.

He could just abandon this fool's errand and go back to the stunning island.

But Drake didn't give up. That was his blessing and his curse.

It was his vice and his virtue.

"Can't," Drake said as he passed the captain. "There's something I have to do."

The man nodded.

"I'm usually here every other week, stay about an hour or so. If you've got the money, I'll take you back."

Drake acknowledged the comment, then stepped over several rotting boards as he made his way to shore. He'd just reached a gnarly looking bush with thorns the size of his baby finger when he heard someone shout.

"Wait up! Hey! *El phantasmo,* wait up!"

Drake turned to see the man on the boat who'd handed him the liquor hurrying toward him.

"My name's Drake—I don't care much for *el phantasmo,*" he said when the man, who was several inches shorter and about twenty pounds lighter than himself, reached his side.

The man blinked at him several times and then held out his hand. It was an awkward introduction given that they'd already met, but Drake went along with it.

"Diego," the man said. They shook hands, then stared at one another for several more seconds. Then, without prompting, Diego turned and pointed to an area of brush off to the right.

"Come, we go dis way."

Before Drake could reply, Diego was off, moving seamlessly over the rotten dock. Like with the other Colombians, as soon as the man stepped into the brush, the foliage seemed to close behind him like some sort of organic door.

Drake took one more look back at the captain, who was still staring at him with those red-rimmed eyes, before turning back to the jungle.

"Fuck it," he whispered with a shrug before hurrying after Diego.

***

If it hadn't been for Diego, Drake could have easily seen himself wandering aimlessly in the jungle until he perished from dehydration and heatstroke. But the little Colombian was like some sort of bush ninja, dodging and weaving branches and shrubbery alike, following secret, organic road signs that only he could see. And, huffing and puffing as he tried to keep up, Drake emerged from the thicket less than an hour later.

"What the hell?"

The change in scenery was so sudden, that he actually looked back the way he'd come just to make sure that this wasn't some sort of mirage.

And Diego was still there, grinning at him.

"We going here," he said, pointing at a small, concrete building that had what looked like a first-generation air-conditioning unit hanging out a wooden opening in the wall.

Normally, Drake would have protested —*in and out, I'm here for two reasons, that's it*—but he was so damn hot that just the idea of air-conditioning was enough to give him a chill. Not that it would have mattered anyway; Diego was off again, bounding toward the building.

A few seconds later, the man was holding the door open for him, still smiling broadly. With cool air spilling out, Drake picked up his pace and stepped inside.

Even though it took several seconds for his eyes to adjust to the dim interior, he didn't need to see to know what sort of establishment he found himself in.

In New York City, Montreal, Mexico, and even Colombia, it seemed, the characteristic sounds of a bar were all the same: muted chatter, terrible music, and the occasional clinking of glasses.

Diego led the way to a small table and took a seat. Drake slid into the booth across from him.

"*El phantasmo*, you want to drink?"

Drake wiped his forehead with his palm and was surprised to see that his hand was shaking.

That was answer enough; Diego whistled and raised a hand high in the air. That too, it appeared, was universal.

Chapter 19

Screech shook his head.

"You've got to be kidding me. You have to be *fucking* kidding me."

Sgt. Yasiv pressed his lips together and mimicked Screech's head movements.

"I'm not."

Furious, Screech looked over at Hanna who simply shrugged. Leroy, on the other hand, had a strange, bewildered expression on his face; the boy looked out of his depth, mostly because he *was* out of his depth.

They *all* were.

"Please tell me this is a joke. After all we've been through? Leroy almost getting shot in the face, Drake nearly mauled to death in prison, Hanna nearly murdered by a serial killer, and—"

"Well, he didn't really try to—"

Screech ignored Hanna and continued in a rapid clip.

"—and I was nearly blown up by a maniac with an assault rifle. And for what? You're telling me that that's *still* not enough to end this? That we still have to be involved in this crazy shit?"

Yasiv's tone was calm and even, and yet Screech detected anger buried deep down.

"Ken's not coming back to New York—I doubt we'll ever see him again. But, if by some chance he does return, we've got more than enough to put him behind bars for a long time. As for Raul? He'll cave, plead out. Get fifteen, serve two-thirds. Palmer and the other cops are trying to work the legal system to their advantage, but they're not going anywhere, either. The DA is desperately trying to hold onto his job, and the only way to do that is to make sure these corrupt bastards see some jail time; *real* jail time. And we know what happens to cops in prison."

As he spoke, Yasiv pulled a worn sheet of paper out of his pocket and slowly unfolded it. Then he held it out to Screech, but he refused to take it.

He knew what it was, whose names were on it.

"No, no way," Screech said, shaking his head again. "We got everybody on that list. We got everybody who mattered. Horatio is dead. Ken is on the run. Raul is in chains. Ray Reynolds? Dead. That Russian sex trafficker fuck? Also dead."

"There's still one more; there's still Steffani Loomis."

Screech threw his hands up in frustration. He couldn't believe this; he thought that this was behind him, that never again would he have to hear about *ANGUIS Holdings* or the Church of Liberation or any of this shit.

With Ken gone, he'd figured that the last peg would just fall into place. After all, shit flowed downstream, didn't it?

"*You* go after Steffani. Use all your manpower in the NYPD and *you* go after her."

Yasiv exhaled loudly.

"I can't."

"And why the fuck not?"

"Because she's connected."

Screech looked to the heavens and opened his mouth in a silent scream.

"Look, her dad is high up in the military. I can't go after her, but you can... so long as there is one high-ranking member of ANGUIS Holdings left—"

"I don't care."

"I'm telling you, Screech. This entity that Ken set up... it really is a snake. A fucking venomous snake."

Screech glared at him.

"Snake? *Snake?* This goddamn thing is more like a fuckin' worm; you cut off a little piece of the worm, and it just keeps on living. Even though after we've cut into—what? Four? Five pieces?—it just keeps on living. When is this ever going to *stop*?"

"Well, technically, a worm can only survive if you cut it above the clitellum. Even then, only one—"

"Shut up, Leroy," Screech snapped. Even before the word had come out of his mouth, he regretted it. "Shit... sorry. I just thought... I just thought we were done with all this shit."

He took a deep breath and massaged his forehead.

I wish... I wish I let my brother go to prison and never had to cut a deal and take this goddamn job.

"Me too," Yasiv said softly. "Me too."

After several seconds of silence, Yasiv pulled a plastic bag out of his pocket and held it out to Leroy.

Screech barely noticed this interaction; he was still fuming about the prospect of being dragged back into this mess.

"Wait—is that... is that Declan's chain?" Leroy asked.

Yasiv nodded.

"Yeah. Managed to get it out of evidence. Take it."

Leroy swallowed hard and reached for the plastic bag. He had tears in his eyes as he looked through the plastic at the gold chain.

"Thank you," he said softly. "Thanks for—"

"What can we even do about this, Yasiv? In case you haven't noticed, Drake's not here and none of us are even registered PIs."

Yasiv turned back to Screech, his face hardening again. Then he reached into his pocket for what felt like the thousandth time and pulled out three wallet-sized ID badge holders. He handed one to each of them.

"Yeah, I figured you might say that. I managed to pull a few strings, fudge the requirements given what you guys did in the Ken Smith case—not everyone was under his spell. This also means you guys can carry, by the way, except for you, Leroy."

Screech didn't even bother looking at the ID.

"It doesn't matter; we're tapped out here. We spent all our money getting this place up and running, and now you tell us that we need to take on a woman whose father is in the military? Do we—" Screech gestured to the three of them, realizing how inept they appeared, —"look like we're capable of something like that?"

Yasiv shrugged.

"I've seen you do more with less, to be honest." Screech opened his mouth to protest, but Yasiv held up a hand, silencing him. "Dunno, Screech. I'm just telling you the way it is. Ken might be gone and the network that he used to distribute his product is destroyed, but so long as ANGUIS still exists, so long as Steffani's still around, things will eventually go back to the way they were; regress to the mean. And when they do, what do you think is going to happen to this shop you have here? To DSLGB Investigations or whatever you call yourself? People know what you guys did. People know, and they'll come for you."

Screech had had enough; the sergeant's words were bordering on a threat now. And while he might be nothing like Drake, Screech didn't take kindly to threats, either.

"That's it," he said under his breath.

"I came here to help, to —"

"That's it!" Screech suddenly shouted. "Get out!"

"Screech, maybe—" Hanna began, but Screech was having none of it.

"Yasiv, *get the fuck out!*"

Yasiv just stared at him for a moment, the outer corners of his eyes drooping just a little. For a second, Screech felt sorry for the man. After all, he'd put everything on the line to bring down ANGUIS, as well.

But they'd still given more; the namesakes of DLSH Investigations had given nearly everything.

"Get out!"

Yasiv didn't need to be told a fourth time. He spun around and quickly left the room.

When he was gone, and the door was closed behind him, the three of them just stood there in silence.

And then Screech cursed and yanked the desk drawer open.

"Well?" he asked, holding up the bottle of Johnny Blue. "What the hell are you waiting for? Get some goddamn glasses."

Chapter 20

THE BEER HELPED COOL DRAKE down. It also helped to stop his hand from shaking.

Only after he'd downed half the glass of some no-name beer did Drake take the opportunity to look around. This was no tourist bar; that much was obvious. In fact, he was the only gringo in sight. It helped, he supposed, that he hadn't shaved in well over a month and that there were still hints of the bruises on his face from the beating he'd taken in prison; and yet it felt like everybody in the room was staring at him, nonetheless.

"Where is it that you want to go, *el phantasmo*?" Diego said finally, sipping his own beer.

Drake hated that name, but he'd also given up trying to convince the man to just call him Drake.

"I'm looking for somebody."

Diego nodded.

"Another gringo."

Drake concurred.

On a whim, he pulled out the photograph that he'd shown the maître d' back in the Virgin Gorda. Diego studied it for several moments before speaking up.

"It's a lot nicer than the boat we came in on," he remarked.

Drake smirked. Indeed, a *lot* nicer.

"I've seen it before—on the news," he continued. "It burned down."

"Yeah, I saw that, too. They said my brother was on it, but nothing was ever sent to me or any of my family in New York. If he was on the boat, I want to see his body."

The words came out with surprisingly little emotion. With all that had happened with Ken Smith, he'd had no time to properly grieve for his brother. Drake had simply compartmentalized his death in an area of his brain to access later.

And yet, it *was* later, and he was still unfettered by the idea that Dane was dead.

Drake wasn't sure if this was because he held out hope that his brother was still alive somewhere, that he'd just disappeared as the man had done all those years ago, or if he'd just lost the ability to *feel*.

Drake grabbed his beer and took a mouthful of the malted water.

"Maybe he's still alive," he said after swallowing, but it was unclear if he was trying to convince Diego or himself.

The man across from him downed his own beer then signaled for the waiter to bring another round. When the drinks arrived, Drake reached into his pocket for the few American dollars he had left, but Diego beat him to it.

"This one's on me. You should drink up—you'll need your strength."

Drake's eyes narrowed.

"For what?"

"For your brother, because I know where he is. It's a long walk from here. Drink, then we'll go see him."

Chapter 21

TOGETHER, HANNA AND SCREECH FINISHED off more than a third of the bottle of Johnny Walker Blue. Leroy was more interested in his brother's chain than the booze, which was just as well, given his age.

"*WWDD?*" Hanna said, lifting her glass and staring at the golden liquid. "What the fuck would Damien Drake do?"

"He's not Jesus," Screech grumbled, before finishing his drink.

"No, he's definitely not *that*."

"Because if he was, he could've walked to Colombia, instead of asking to borrow ten grand to get there."

"He really is there, isn't he? Chasing down Ken Smith?" Hanna asked.

Screech shrugged.

"Honestly? I don't know where he is."

"I doubt he'd give up, and as much as it annoys me to say this, I don't think we should, either. I mean, I wasn't here in the beginning, when this all started, but don't we owe it to him to see this through? After all, it's his name on the door, isn't it?"

"No, not anymore; it's *our* names on the door," Screech corrected.

"You know what I mean."

Screech wanted to disagree with her but couldn't bring himself to do it. She was right, in a way. They owed him. After all they'd sacrificed along the way, Screech couldn't imagine it being for naught, of ANGUIS Holdings eventually returning to power.

There was also something to be said for completeness, finality.

Thoughts of what Drake might do should he accomplish the nearly impossible task of hunting down Ken Smith in Colombia came to mind, which instantly reminded him of another person who was there in the beginning: Beckett.

Beckett had his own ideas of finality.

Screech shuddered involuntarily then reached out and refilled his glass.

There was another reason for wanting to put an end to all this, aside from the moral and ethical implications. Steffani Loomis and ANGUIS Holdings was the final string that held him to Drake. As much as he owed the man, as much as he *liked* the man—most of the time, anyway—Screech also wanted to be free of the spiderweb that seemed to govern his very movements.

And the only way to do that? Oh, why all they had to do was just take down a high-ranking military officer and his daughter.

Screech sighed.

"Fuck… How do we even go about doing this? Any ideas? I don't even know who Steffani Loomis is, where she lives, what she does. Nothing."

Leroy cleared his throat.

"We can find out, look into if she has any sort of online presence, social media, that sort of thing. I'm guessing that she's not posting selfies with bricks of heroin, but there'll be a history, a trail."

Hanna nodded in agreement.

"You know, I once worked as an executive assistant to the CEO of a hospital. A new hire, this man was the charismatic leader that the hospital needed. They were looking to break ground on a new site, but the government was dragging its feet. So, the Board of Directors brought this man in knowing that he would do whatever it takes to get things moving. And you wanna know what he did?"

"Quit?"

Hanna rolled her eyes.

"He broke ground himself. Literally; one day, the man, who was built like a penguin, by the way, got a shovel out and just started digging."

Screech sighed.

"What's your point, Hanna?"

"Well, anyways, to make a long story short, the hospital got built, but the CEO wasn't doing it out of the goodness of his heart. He'd organized a kickback of ten or eleven million dollars from the construction company they hired to finish the job. But here's the thing: as soon as all this came to light? The embezzlement? The fraud? Everyone around the CEO, everyone who had previously sung the man's praises — friends, politicians, the Board of Directors themselves — they immediately distanced themselves from him. It was like he was the black fucking plague. It didn't matter what they'd said before, how close they were, they just lied through their teeth to try to stay afloat the sinking ship."

Screech chewed the inside of his lip, finally understanding the analogy.

"So, let me guess, whatever's left of ANGUIS Holdings, including Steffani Loomis, is going to be doing everything in their power to distance themselves from Ken Smith."

Hanna nodded glumly.

"Right on, Durango. That's exactly what happened. But... *but*, while they did everything they could to stay away from the CEO, the relationships between one another just grew stronger. You know how Drake kept rambling about power as a driving motivator for these people? Well, these fucking people didn't see this as a time to clean up their act, but a time to grab the power that was left in the CEO's wake. It's what brought them all down in the end."

Screech and Leroy waited for Hanna to continue, but she just looked at them.

"…that's what brought them down, in the *end*," she repeated after a few moments. "…*end*. That's it. All I got. What the hell are you waiting for? Why are you staring at me like that?"

It was Leroy who spoke up first.

"You were an executive assistant? *You?*"

Screech chuckled; he couldn't help himself, mostly because he was thinking the same thing. He couldn't picture this woman, this woman who had multiple piercings in her ears and used to have her head half-shaved, being subservient to anyone. Probably, the CEO was working for *her*, only he didn't know it.

"Fuck off."

"Okay, okay, easy now," Screech said. "So, what are you saying? You're saying that we should find out what country club all these rich and powerful people hang out in and infiltrate them, MI6 style?"

Hanna stared at him blankly.

"Nothing gets by you, Ken Jennings."

"Yeah, no offense, but I definitely don't fit in that crowd, and I don't think either of you does, either," Leroy offered. "And I'm thinking you can't just waltz up to the golf course and ask for a membership."

Screech frowned. The boy was right.

"Well, let me ask you something," Hanna said as she poured herself another drink. "Back when you guys were just the old Triple D, you didn't happen to have any rich people on your Rolodex, did you?"

Screech sipped his scotch.

"No, we didn't. Shit, the only clients we had was some corrupt sex ring smuggler who looked like Dorian Yates, and some old—"

Screech stopped cold.

"What?" Leroy asked. "What is it?"

"Just a second."

Screech spun around and started typing on his keyboard. Eventually, a single name appeared on the screen.

"Mrs. Armatridge?" Hanna asked, leaning over his shoulder. "Who the hell is Mrs. Armatridge?"

"Our ticket to the ball, that's who," Screech replied in a phony Southern accent. "And I think that you might just be the *debutante* that everyone is waiting to see."

Chapter 22

"THIS IS THE SPOT," DIEGO said, before indicating for the driver to pull over to the side of the road.

Drake, who had been dozing during the hour or so car ride, sat bolt upright and immediately tried to soak in his surroundings. He was still a little wary of Diego's motives—nobody was this helpful without wanting something in return—but he had no one else to rely on in this foreign land. But now, as he stared out at a squat building labeled as *Centro Médico* followed by the iconic symbol of the two snakes winding around a winged staff, he gave his head a serious shake.

What the hell are we doing here? What the hell am I doing here?

Drake had had a lot of time on the boat to think about this, of course, but then he'd been driven by rage and the prospect of revenge. Now, sharing a cab with a man he'd only just met, the reality of how daunting a task he'd embarked on—searching for two gringos in a country roughly twice the size of Texas—hit him like a ton of bricks.

What in the fuck am I doing here?

He'd come to Colombia with a handful of extra clothes, a small amount of cash, and that was pretty much it. Shit, he didn't even speak Spanish. The one thing he did know, however, the one thing he was confident about was that he didn't usually have to go far to look for trouble.

In fact, it usually found him.

"My brother's here?" Drake asked as he stepped out of the cab. The sun was still high in the sky, and the air was impossibly hot; just breathing was painful. It wasn't all that different from being choked out by Rodney Wise in prison.

"*Jes*; this is it," Diego said, appearing at his side. "Come—I do the talking, *jes*?"

Drake shrugged.

"*Jes*—look, I'm just here to see my brother. I'm not sure if they have a database of names, or photographs, or..."

Diego shook his head.

"This place keeps lots of bodies that haven't been... claimed. They don't have names. You have to go in and search for yourself."

Drake struggled to catch up with the man. He was short, but he moved like some sort of spider.

"How... how do you know all this?"

Even from behind, he could see the man's shoulders slump and knew the answer before Diego spoke.

"I've been here before," he said quietly.

Drake was inclined to ask more, but they were stopped by a security guard just inside the double doors of *Centro Médico*. Sporting a uniform that was the same shade as the building's cracked foundation, the man was at least six and a half feet tall, with broad lips, and a shaved head. Drake watched a curious exchange between the two men; despite being nearly a foot taller than Diego, it was the former who seemed intimidated. Eventually, the security guard bowed his head and stepped off to one side.

Drake made a mental note to ask Diego what he'd said to the guard later. Right now, he had to hustle just to keep up with the man; he was off again, hurrying toward a filthy desk with an enormous woman sitting behind it. They passed maybe a dozen or so people sitting in chairs off to one side, people with sunken eyes and heavy chins, but Diego paid them no heed. He waltzed right up to the desk like he owned the place, and then barked something in Spanish. The woman leaned forward on her perch to get a better look at Drake, her chair squealing in protest. The two of them locked eyes until Drake eventually turned to Diego to make sure that he wasn't supposed to say something, answer a question, perhaps. But then the woman's scarlet lips twisted into a half-hearted smile, and she aimed a pudgy finger, adorned with a claw-like nail with polish that matched her lip color, down the hall.

The security guard reappeared, following closely behind Diego and Drake as they made their way down a narrow hallway and passed through a set of swinging doors.

"Diego? Are you sure that—"

The guard hushed him. Drake frowned but decided that it was in his best interest not to get on the man's bad side; not here, anyway.

They continued in silence, passing doors on either side of the hall marked only by large, bold numbers. None of them had any windows.

Is this some sort of... asylum?

In a way, *Centro Médico* reminded Drake a little of Oak Valley Psychiatric Institution. Although this place lacked the level of security of the building he'd called home for a short while, it shared the same suffocating loneliness. Just as this memory threatened to evoke a visceral reaction in Drake, they came to a door that was propped open with a wooden wedge.

Even though something in the back of his mind warned him against looking in, temptation got the better of Drake.

"Jesus," he whispered. The sound echoed off the walls in such a way that Drake felt momentarily dizzy.

Inside the room were dozens of bodies haphazardly laid atop gurneys, some of which weren't even covered with sheets. Pale gray skin and grizzly black hair stood out on the faces of the dead.

Drake swallowed hard and put a hand against the wall in order to steady himself.

Dane's here? No... he... he can't be...

An odor suddenly filled the hallway, but it wasn't the scent of blood or decay, as Drake might expect, but the strong, stringent smell of preservatives.

It made his nose crinkle and his mind swim.

Diego continued ahead, but Drake couldn't seem to take his eyes off the bodies in the room. Until a hand came down and gripped his shoulder, that is.

His first instinct was to whip around, and he did try, but the grip was incredibly strong and held him in place. Drake caught a glimpse of the security guard's stern face before the man shoved him forward.

"Fuck," Drake muttered, barely managing to stay on his feet. "Some welcoming committee you are."

Diego, who was oblivious to this interaction, hollered over his shoulder. The sound was so loud that Drake had to resist the urge to cover his ears like a child.

"Room eleven."

Although Drake had since regained his senses, as he passed room eight and nine, his breath started to quicken, and his pace slowed.

He was no stranger to death, and he wasn't particularly close with his brother, but Drake couldn't help but think that this was his fault, that he'd somehow dragged Dane into this mess.

It wasn't true, of course; Ken had wanted Dane because of his connections in South America, Colombia, even.

But Ken also wanted me. And he knew that if he recruited me, I could bring in Dane.

Diego stopped outside door eleven and gestured to the handle with his hand. Drake, moving very slowly now, walked up next to him and took a deep breath.

I shouldn't be here. Fuck, I should have never come here. I should be home with Jasmine and Clay and Screech and everyone else. I shouldn't be here.

But that didn't change the fact that he *was* here.

Drake ground his teeth and reached for the door handle, only to instinctively pull back.

It was freezing cold.

"Door eleven," Diego repeated, sounding as if he were miles away now.

"Yeah, I heard you," Drake mumbled, grabbing the handle again. This time, he ignored the frosty bite and pulled it wide.

He sighed in relief when he wasn't greeted by a valley of corpses. But his relief soon became confusion.

Not only were there no bodies in the room, but there was *nothing* in the room.

It was completely empty.

"He's not here," Drake said, stating the obvious. "My brother's not—"

He started to turn, but only made it halfway before something thick and heavy was draped over his head and cinched tight.

Chapter 23

"HOUSE ARREST? WHAT ARE YOU talking about, house arrest?" Screech nearly shouted into the phone.

Roger Schneiderman cleared his throat.

"I can't really discuss anything else, Screech. You know, lawyer-client confidentiality and all that."

Screech shook his head.

This conversation was turning out to be even stranger than Yasiv's visit.

The only person he knew who had connections with the elite of New York was Mrs. Armatridge. And, given the fact that they'd worked together previously, and that it had been none other than Ken Smith who had referred her to them, Screech figured that he might be able to leverage this 'relationship.'

What he hadn't expected was for his call to be forwarded to the very same lawyer Screech had used to represent both Leroy and Drake. And the icing on the cake was that Mrs. Armatridge wasn't able to use the phone right now because she was on house arrest and had already used up her privileges for the day.

Could it be possible that she was involved in ANGUIS Holdings as well? Was she part of the fallout from the Ken Smith saga?

Screech didn't think so—he didn't remember hearing her name mentioned—but he couldn't be certain; Yasiv had told them that more than a hundred indictments had been passed down since Ken fled the country.

He covered the bottom of the phone with his hand.

"Leroy, see if you can find out anything about Mrs. Armatridge's current legal issues online."

The man nodded and turned to his computer.

"All right, thanks, Roger," Screech said after pulling his hand away from the phone. He waited several seconds for a sign-off that never came. "Roger? You still there?"

"Yeah, I'm here; listen, it's about the retainer, Screech. As you know, Drake's legal troubles are, umm, *ongoing*. If you want to keep me on retainer, I'm going to need another payment shortly."

Screech massaged his temples. While what he'd said to Yasiv wasn't completely true—they hadn't blown *all* their capital renting and modifying their new offices—money was indeed tight. His money man, Banksy, had done an exceptional job turning the cash he'd received for recovering *B-Yacht'ch* into a princely sum. But what with bailing out Drake, and then paying for Leroy's court fees… they were spread fairly thin.

"All right, I'll look into it."

"Yeah, well it's just that you're already a month in arrears and I have—"

"I said, I'd look into it. Look, I've got a lot on my plate right now. I'll get back to you. Promise."

Before the man could argue further, Screech hung up the phone. Then he tapped it absently against his palm.

Why are you paying for Drake's legal bills, Screech? he asked himself. *He received half of the money for the yacht job, and yet you're shelling out all the cash for the company. Shit, you even had to lend him money for him to sneak his ass out of the US and into Colombia. Why can't he—*

"Screech? You alright?"

Screech looked up.

"Hmm?"

"I asked if you were okay," Leroy said with a frown. "You just looked a little—"

"Fine. I'm fine. Did you find out anything about Mrs. Armatridge?"

Leroy just stared at him for a moment longer, one eyebrow raised.

Screech clapped his hands and the man snapped out of it.

"Yeah, I… I think? If this is the same person… well, you're not gonna believe this, but your lady friend has been indicted."

In his mind, he pictured the blue-haired woman with the upturned nose and pearls around her neck. Sure, she'd been bossy and ornery, but indicted?

"Really? For what?"

Leroy swallowed hard and when he finally answered, Screech nearly fell out of his chair.

"For murder."

Chapter 24

"TRY TO STAY CALM," DIEGO instructed.

But that was like telling an ant to remain still in a rainstorm.

Drake had some sort of bag over his head and his hands were bound behind him. He thrashed violently and kicked at whoever was holding him, which, given the sheer strength of the grip was likely the massive security guard. Before he knew what was happening, there were more hands on him now, and he was hoisted off the ground and flipped so that he was perpendicular to the cracked ceramic floor that he could no longer see. But this didn't deter Drake's struggles; if anything, he redoubled his efforts. He managed to drive his right foot into something soft and he heard someone grunt. For a moment, there was more room for him to move freely, and he entertained the idea of planting his feet and running away from this nightmare.

But the hands returned, squeezing him even tighter now. The next thing he knew, his ankles were zip-tied like his hands, and Drake found himself tightly wrapped like meat in a casing.

"Stay calm," Diego repeated. The man's voice was muffled, but it was impossible to tell if this was because he had also been captured, or if the bag on his head was just filtering the sound.

"Let me fucking go," he shouted back, continuing to thrash.

Something struck him in the stomach then, blasting the air from him and crushing his lungs.

He gaped and gasped furiously, but his body wouldn't respond, wouldn't suck in a fresh breath. Blood roared in his ears and his eyes bulged so far from his head that he could have sworn he felt the coarse fabric brush against his corneas.

What the fuck is going on? his mind screamed.

"Drake, if you want to live, you'll be calm."

And that was when he knew that it was a setup. Somehow, Raul or Ken must have gotten wind of his trip to Colombia and had put someone on the boat to keep him in line.

And that someone just happened to be the friendly Colombian who went by the name of Diego.

Once again, Drake's lack of planning had come back to haunt him.

At long last, just moments before he thought he might pass out, he managed to reinflate his lungs.

The sound was horrible, like the death throes of an asphyxiating bullfrog. But in moments, his mind started to clear, and then he immediately set about trying to count the number of men who were holding him.

He felt at least four sets of hands, two of which could have only belonged to the security guard. Two others were smaller than the rest, likely belonging to Diego.

Four men… I've had worse odds.

Except he usually wasn't zip-tied and blindfolded.

He heard someone shout in Spanish before a door was thrown wide. The hot Colombian sun beat down on him, causing sweat to immediately break out on his forehead. There was a squeal of tires and he smelled diesel fuel in the air.

"*Dentro! Dentro!*"

Diego's voice.

Drake was suddenly airborne.

"What the—"

He landed hard on his right arm, and that side of his body clenched; his liver, sensitive as it was, decided that right about now was the time to revolt.

The pain Drake felt was so intense that he gagged and almost threw up. He knew, however, that if he gave in to this urge, he'd likely drown on his own puke.

By some miracle, he managed to swallow the bile back down.

The door slammed closed somewhere at his feet, and the truck or van or whatever it was that he was in, peeled off again.

Gritting his teeth against the pain, Drake tried to sit up but found that the best he could do was roll onto his left side. Gasping for air, he listened, trying to gain some insight into the men who had kidnapped him.

But all he could make out was the roar of the engine.

"Where are you taking me?" he demanded.

A hand came down on his shoulder, sparking new pain, and Drake ineffectively tried to roll away from his assailant.

"Drake, be calm. You need to be calm. *Calma.*"

Drake did the opposite; he thrust his feet back so far that they whacked against the wall. When he felt this resistance, he kicked again and again, generating a metallic drum roll.

"*Calma!*"

In addition to Diego's voice, others were shouting now, too, yelling things in Spanish that Drake didn't comprehend.

"Drake, please, you must—"

Another hand on his shoulder, only this time the grip was nearly crushing. Drake continued to kick as even more hands desperately tried to hold him still.

Something sharp pierced his right bicep, and he cried out.

"Let go! *Let me fucking go! Let me—*"

Someone grabbed the cord fastening the bag to his head and pulled tight. Drake's head was yanked back, and he had no choice but to finally stop kicking.

A cord of some sort dug deep into his throat, cutting off his air supply. He gasped, once, twice, then everything went dark.

Chapter 25

SCREECH WAS SURPRISED WHEN MRS. Armatridge's door was opened not by herself or by Roger Schneiderman, but by a man he'd never seen before.

A man who looked none too happy to see him.

"Yes?" he said, a frown on his heavy-lined face.

"Yes, uh, hi," Screech began, shoving his hands deep into his pockets as he spoke. It was all he could do to keep his eyes on the man and not look down at his toes. "I'm here to see Mrs. Armatridge?"

The man's brow furrowed, his overgrown eyebrows becoming a single caterpillar snaking across his leathery forehead.

"Mrs. Armatridge isn't taking visitors at this time."

Screech tried to peer over the man's shoulder, but Lurch shifted his thin frame to block his view.

"Can you just give her a message then? Tell her that Screech came by?"

The man made a face, one that suggested he'd do nothing of the sort, before starting to close the door.

"Please? Tell her it's Screech, tell her that I work…*ed* for Triple D Investigations."

When the butler or whatever the hell he was didn't even acknowledge this last comment, Screech became desperate.

"Mrs. Armatridge," he nearly shouted into the ever-narrowing opening. "Mrs. Armatridge! It's about Drake!"

Just before the door closed completely in his face, a woman's voice filtered through to him.

"Let him in," Mrs. Armatridge said, her voice completely devoid of emotion. The butler didn't immediately open the door, but he did stop closing it, which was something. When

Mrs. Armatridge repeated the order, his face turned sour, and he reluctantly pulled the door wide and stepped aside.

"Thanks, Jeeves," Screech grumbled as he stepped inside the estate.

He'd been here once before with Drake, setting up surveillance equipment to spy on the woman's husband, but that had been so long ago that he'd forgotten just how majestic it truly was.

The walls were adorned with gilded paintings, the ceilings extended into the stratosphere, and the wainscoting on the walls looked to have been carved from the bones of some prehistoric beast. Screech was just trying to take this all in when a voice challenged him from his right.

"What about Drake?"

Screech put on a placating smile and turned his attention to Mrs. Armatridge, who was seated in a suede loveseat just beside the front door. The woman was wearing a soft pink blouse, with some sort of paisley cravat covering her throat. The left ankle of her white slacks bulged slightly, successfully disguising the ankle monitor hidden beneath.

"Yes, Mrs. Armatridge, I'm sorry that I—"

The woman waved a hand adorned with a half-dozen rings of varying sizes.

"Get on with it. What is this about Drake?"

Screech took a deep breath, a clear stall tactic as he tried to segue into the real reason why he was here.

"Ah, I see; you lied," Mrs. Armatridge said, immediately cluing into what was going on here. She turned to Lurch and gave him a curt nod. "Darren, can you please see our guest out?"

The butler was much quicker than his age suggested, and his subsequent grip on Screech's shoulder was strong.

"No, wait; I'm sorry. I just... I just, uh, I need your help."

Mrs. Armatridge raised a finely penciled eyebrow and nodded at Darren. While the butler didn't release Screech's shoulder completely, he loosened his grip.

"The only reason that I allowed you to enter my home is because you're a friend of Drake's. What I'm confused about, child, is why you are asking me for help, when, instead, you should be offering to do something for me."

Screech was tired and still a little hazy from all the Johnny Blue he'd consumed back in their new headquarters, and the woman's words confused him.

"I don't know... I'm not sure what..."

The woman teased up her trouser leg and displayed the ankle monitor.

"Based on the money that I've paid you for your services, as well as the clientele that I've sent your way, one would safely assume that this is a house call—that Triple D or whatever you call yourself is checking up on me to see if there's anything I need? Anything at all?"

The woman's piercing blue eyes darted down to the ankle monitor then back up to Screech's.

Things suddenly became clear; Leroy had debriefed him about Mrs. Armatridge's case—she was under indictment for murdering her husband—but it was the woman's careful choice of words that gave her away.

All her wealth was tied up in lawyers and bail and she needed someone, someone to do her dirty work.

In short, she needed someone like Screech.

"I would like to be rid of this tacky thing, as I would like to be rid of these ridiculous charges that are hanging over my head."

Screech nodded.

"You're right, Mrs. Armatridge; you were instrumental in helping Drake and I form our practice. And I do believe that we owe you. But this... the charges you are facing are serious."

Mrs. Armatridge rolled her eyes.

"Yes, of course, they are serious — don't be simple with me. We both know that if it weren't for the DA desperately trying to save his job, none of this nonsense would ever be happening. Still, you'd think that he had more important things to focus on than to sic an old helpless lady with trumped-up charges."

Old lady you may be, Mrs. Armatridge, Screech thought, *but helpless you are not.*

And yet, he found his eyes drifting to a wheelchair located not far from where Mrs. Armatridge sat.

He couldn't remember her needing that before. Mrs. Armatridge must have noticed his gaze because she addressed the issue immediately.

"See? I'm basically wheelchair-bound, and they claim that I pushed poor Armand *up* the stairs? Ridiculous."

Screech assessed the woman for a moment before continuing.

His previous thought held true; wheelchair-bound or ambulatory, this woman was far from helpless.

"Ok, fine. Enough games. I have a few friends I can speak to about your charges, about the case. But there's something I need in return."

Mrs. Armatridge frowned.

"If it's money you seek, your request will have to wait until after this legal nonsense is resolved."

"No, it's not money. It's something else. A *sensitive* matter." Screech cast a glance over his shoulder at Darren the butler.

Mrs. Armatridge dismissed the man with another nod.

"Well, get on with it. If not money, what is it that you want?"

"I need a ticket," Screech said without hesitation.

Mrs. Armatridge's frown deepened.

"A ticket? What kind of ticket?"

"Why, a ticket to the ball, of course. A very prestigious and exclusive ball."

Chapter 26

TIME HAD A WAY OF dilating and contracting when your senses were occluded and being drugged just exacerbated this effect. Which was why, when Drake finally awoke with a splitting headache reminiscent of one of his more epic hangovers, he had no idea how much time had passed.

What he was certain of, however, was that he was no longer in a vehicle. At some point, his captors must have carried his limp body somewhere else. Drake now found himself in a seated position, propped up against a wall. It was thankfully cool here, and that, combined with the fact that he was inundated with the smell of earth, suggested that he was in some sort of basement.

Or dungeon; he could be in a dungeon, for all he knew.

His hands and ankles were still bound, but Drake was surprised that his liver had since taken a break from its revolution. It appeared as if whatever Diego and his crew had injected him with also had an analgesic effect.

What a bunch of nice guys... just stand-up, genuinely kind individuals.

Drake grunted and shifted his head against the hard wall, trying to tease the hood off. But, to his dismay, he quickly realized that it was still tightly fastened around his throat.

"Hello?" he croaked. "Anyone there?"

Movement from his left drew his attention. He turned his head in that direction, only to have it locked in place by two strong hands.

Drake knew better than to resist this time.

He heard a snap, then felt pressure on his shins. Another snap.

Whoever was in the dungeon with him had just severed the tie that bound his ankles and the one that held the bag on his head.

Drake grunted as he stretched his legs, then the hood was yanked off him and he blinked rapidly.

It took a few seconds for all the sweat and grime to clear from his eyes so that he could properly make out the figure squatting before him.

It was Diego, and he looked about as happy as Drake felt in that moment.

"I told you to be calm," the man said as he jammed a set of pliers into the pocket of his filthy jeans. "*Calma.*"

Drake turned his head to the side and spat.

"My bad," he grunted. Every word he spoke seemed to inflate his head, ratchet the PSI in his skull up a few points. The drugs he'd been injected with had stopped working when they'd reached his solar plexus, it seemed.

Diego's mouth was a thin line.

"I didn't want to do this, *el phantasmo.*"

Drake blinked more sweat from his eyes.

"Why the fuck do you keep calling me that? Why do you keep calling me a goddamn ghost?"

"Because at first, I thought you were *him.*"

Drake shook his head.

"What? Who?"

"Dane… I thought you were Dane."

It suddenly all made sense to Drake. He recalled the way Diego had looked at him on the boat as if he'd seen him before. And then there was the maître d' on the Virgin Gorda, who had been overcome by confusion at his appearance.

Diego called him a ghost because he thought he was Dane.

And Dane was dead.

"Well, I'm not him. Now, how about you let me go?"

Diego suddenly rose to his feet and gestured down the hallway to someone that Drake couldn't see.

"Oh, I'm sorry, Drake, but you are even more valuable than your brother. I couldn't believe it when I saw you on the boat... you see, I have a family, one that I wanted to see again. It's... well, let's just say that you are my ticket back. I am sorry, Drake, but as you know, family means everything."

Drake growled and spit again.

"I have no fucking clue what you're talking about. As for family, I—"

A shadow suddenly appeared at the entrance of the cell. One glimpse of the figure and Diego scrambled out of there without another word.

This new man stood tall and, with his head blocking the single overhead bulb, his face was shrouded in darkness.

"Great, another fucking ghoul. Hey, listen, so long as we're going to be friends, how about you give me some more of that drug you injected me with in the van? Hmm? A little pick-me-up between friends. I mean, if I had some—"

The man leaned down, and his features were slowly revealed.

Drake suddenly pushed his back up against the wall.

"What?" he gasped. "You? I thought you were dead."

The man held his hands out to the sides and stared directly into Drake's eyes.

"You thought wrong, Drake. You thought wrong."

Chapter 27

"**WELL? HOW'D IT GO?**" **HANNA** asked as soon as Screech stepped through the door.

"It went… well, it was interesting, that's for sure."

When he offered nothing further, Leroy couldn't help but jump in.

"And? Can Mrs. Armatridge hook us up?"

Instead of answering, Screech pulled an envelope from his pocket and tossed it on Hanna's desk. She quickly opened it and scanned the single sheet of paper within. With her lips starting to curl, she handed the envelope over to an eager Leroy.

"Something tells me that I'm not gonna like this, am I?"

Screech gave her a once-over.

"What's not to like? Good food, good people, *rich* people, and you get to dress up. A win-win… win-win."

Hanna rolled her eyes and shook her head.

"No, I'm *really* not gonna like this."

Leroy shrugged.

"I don't get it. This is… what? An invitation to some sort of auction?"

"Yeah, that's pretty much it," Screech confirmed.

Leroy screwed up his face.

"What? It's an invitation for Mrs. Armatridge, not —" the man's eyes suddenly widened, and he jabbed a finger in Hanna's direction. *"Ohhhhhhh, I get it now… you're* Mrs. Armatridge."

Leroy chuckled, and Screech nodded.

"Yeah, well, Hanna makes a much more convincing Mrs. Armatridge than either you or I."

"Fuckin' hell," Hanna grumbled. "I hate fucking dressing up."

"Hey, don't worry about it, Cinderella. I'll make sure to get you something *purty* to wear to the ball."

Hanna groaned.

"When is this goddamn thing, anyway?"

"Saturday night, which will give us just enough time to figure out our part of the bargain."

"Oh really, there's more? What the hell did you promise the old crust bag, anyway? Your soul?"

"I wish it were that easy. Mrs. Armatridge is in a little legal trouble and she needs our help to wrangle her way out of it."

"Oh, great, so to go along with a now-deceased sex and drug trafficker, Triple D—err, DSLH—is now enlisting a murderer as one of our clients," Hanna remarked.

"Alleged," Screech corrected.

"Yeah, just like Michael Jackson allegedly stuck his—"

"Let's just try to figure this out, shall we?"

Leroy crossed his arms over his chest.

"Well, I doubt that Sgt. Yasiv is about to stick his neck out for us, given how you told him off, oh, about an hour ago."

"Gee, thanks."

"What about your friend in the Coroner's Office?" Hanna suggested.

Screech chewed the inside of his lip. As much as he wanted to stay away from Dr. Beckett Campbell given his suspicions about the man, everything seemed to keep coming back to him.

It wasn't that he was afraid of Beckett, either, because he wasn't. What Screech was really concerned about is what the man might do if it came to light that Mrs. Armatridge was responsible for her husband's death.

Would Beckett take care of her like he took care of Donnie DiMarco? Bob Bumacher? Boris Brackovich?

Screech shuddered.

"Yeah, maybe I'll reach out to him. We've got a few days to think about it, anyway."

"Well, the good news is that I won't be the only one dressing up," Hanna stated, her frown transitioning to a grin.

Screech turned his eyes to the invitation that Leroy still held in his hand.

"No plus ones allowed; sorry, Hanna."

Hanna shook her head.

"Oh, no, I wasn't talking about the debutante ball, but dinner."

Screech's first thought was that Hanna was asking him out on a date and his face started to flush.

"I'm not sure—"

"Oh, god, you're like a horny teenager, aren't you?" Hanna turned to Leroy. "And you, keep quiet. I'm not asking you out, Screech."

Leroy laughed.

"Dinner, at my place," he said.

Screech's confusion only grew.

"What?"

"Well, not technically *my* place, but my mom's. Look, there was nothing I could do about it. She says if I want to work here, not only do I have to finish school, but she wants to meet you guys."

Screech looked skyward.

The last thing he wanted to do was go to Leroy's mom's house for dinner; he had work to do. He had to figure out the Mrs. Armatridge situation, somehow entrap Steffani Loomis, find Drake, and win the lottery to pay Roger Schneiderman.

He had a full plate in front of him, and yet Screech didn't feel all that hungry.

"Please," Leroy pleaded, and Screech gave in. They were partners, after all.

"Okay, fine, but Hanna's coming with."

Hanna grinned.

"But of course; you can be my plus one, sweetheart. But just a heads-up? You're not getting past first base."

Chapter 28

THEY'D ONLY MET A HANDFUL of times, and despite the fact that his hair was longer now, and his skin was deeply tanned, the man before Drake was undoubtedly Wesley Smith.

"I don't know what all the fuss was about. When my dad said that he was going to use you to clean up all the loose ends, to make him a legend in New York City, I had my doubts, my reservations. I guess I was right. And look at you? Pathetic. Useless. *Broken.*"

Drake tried to rise to his feet, but Wesley wagged a finger in his face.

"I wouldn't do that if I were you. You see, things aren't like New York here. In fact, even though I was forced to stay here, I kinda like it. Here, in Colombia, there's accountability. Back in New York, you could pretty much do whatever you wanted and the worst that would happen is that you might get a slap on the wrist, maybe a few months in a country club prison. But here? You see those guys down the hall that brought you in here?" Wesley hesitated. "No, I guess you didn't—you had a bag over your head. Anyways, all I have to do is snap my fingers and any one of them will jump at the opportunity to come over here and cut off some of your bits and feed them to you. Why? Because they know what'll happen to them if they don't listen."

"Where's my brother?" Drake demanded, ignoring everything that Wesley was rambling on about.

"What's with you Drake brothers and slipping through the cracks, huh? I thought I'd dealt with you, even paid off the goddamn judge to make sure that you got jail time for your little stint with Officer Kramer. And your brother? Supposed to be dead, but he's a slippery, slimy bastard, just like you. I guess the rotten apple didn't fall far from the tree."

Drake heard only one thing during the entire diatribe: ...*supposed to be dead*...

Whether he'd intended to or not, Wesley had let it slip that his brother was actually still alive... *somewhere*.

The fire on the yacht had clearly been staged to make it look like both Wesley and Dane had perished when both appeared to be alive.

"Yeah, well I guess in your case, you and your brother are nothing alike," Drake shot back.

The smile slid off Wesley's face and his eyes went dark. He crouched even more and pointed a filthy nail at Drake's face.

"Don't you ever talk about Thomas," he warned.

Drake's brow furrowed.

"What? Are you ashamed of what you and your dad did to him? That you had—"

Wesley pulled his hand back and punched Drake directly between the eyes. The back of his head ricocheted off the cold wall behind him, and stars scattered across his vision. He swooned but somehow managed to remain conscious.

"We didn't do anything to him. It was that sick fuck, Marcus."

Drake spat a wad of blood on the floor and straightened his neck.

And then he smiled.

"You don't even know what your dad did, do you?" Drake said.

Wesley scowled and pulled his fist back again.

"If you say another word, I don't care what Ken wants; I'll kill you myself."

Drake laughed.

"It was your dad, you idiot! He's the one who had Thomas set up, he's the one who got him killed. His own father, your—"

This time the punch struck Drake in the side of the head, and the stars vanished. In their place was a blanket of empty universe that guided him into unconsciousness.

Chapter 29

DURING THE ENTIRE FORTY-MINUTE drive from DSLH Investigations to NYU Medical, a growing sense of anxiety brewed deep within Screech's stomach.

He remembered the first time he really spent any time alone with Dr. Beckett Campbell, Senior Medical examiner for New York State. They were in the Virgin Gorda, and at first, they'd had a good time. He was actually a breath of fresh air, pretty much breaking every stereotype and misconception about doctors in general.

But then things had gotten… *strange*, least of all the two dead models found in his bed.

With Beckett passed out between them.

Screech took a deep breath as he pulled into an empty parking spot. He just sat in his car for a while, trying to decide if there was any possible way to deal with the Mrs. Armatridge situation without involving Beckett.

If there was, he didn't know of any.

A clean break… after DSLH gets this monkey off our back—or snake, as it were—we can do a clean break from all of this, Beckett included. Start over. Fresh.

Screech rubbed his eyes, grateful that last night he'd somehow managed a full six hours of sleep. The alcohol had helped, of course, but it still counted.

Or so he hoped.

Screech quickly made his way down a sterile hallway, eventually arriving at the pathology department. Once there, he was greeted by a secretary sitting behind a large desk. A photograph of the woman with her arm wrapped around Chris Hemsworth was proudly displayed for everyone who approached to see.

"Hi," Screech said, offering his warmest smile. "I'm here to see Dr. Beckett Campbell."

The woman pushed her lips together and then typed away at her keyboard for a moment.

"Is he expecting you? I don't see any appointments on his calendar."

Screech shook his head.

"No, I don't think so. But I'm a friend... my name's Screech and I thought maybe we'd have lunch."

The woman looked at him with a raised eyebrow and then picked up the phone and dialed a number.

The pathology department was so small that Screech actually heard the phone ringing. He followed the sound with his eyes, eventually resting on an office. Even though the door was closed, it was mostly glass and Screech could see right in.

And then things got weird. He half expected to see Beckett behind his desk, but this wasn't the case. The office wasn't unoccupied, either. As he watched, Screech saw a hand snake up from underneath the desk, grope around, then finally grab the receiver before disappearing out of sight again.

Meanwhile, the secretary said something about a visitor, grunted a few times, then hung up.

"I'm sorry," the woman said, drawing Screech's attention, "but Dr. Campbell isn't in right now."

"What? I saw him—he's in his office. I saw his hand."

Screech had to give it to the woman; even in the face of this ridiculous charade, her expression didn't falter.

"Dr. Beckett Campbell's not in today, sir."

"Come on... his hand... look, did you tell him that it was Screech visiting?"

"Dr. Campbell is not in."

Screech rolled his eyes and debated just waltzing over to the man's office and pulling the door open. In the end, he opted for diplomacy; getting arrested wouldn't help DSLH's client prospects any.

"This is ridiculous," he muttered. "Okay, sure, he's not in; do you know when he'll be back, at least?"

"Nuh-uh."

Screech threw his hands up.

"This is insane."

He was about to walk away when he spotted a young woman approaching.

A young woman he recognized.

"Suzan!" he exclaimed. He didn't know the Cuthbert girl very well, but when they had been together, they'd gotten along.

Her head was down, but when she noticed him, her face lit up.

"Screech!"

The woman surprised Screech by reaching out and embracing him. Screech awkwardly hugged back.

"How you been? How's—"

Screech thought that Suzan was going to bring up Drake and he pre-emptively cringed.

He still couldn't believe that the man had abandoned his child and girlfriend to pursue Ken Smith. There had to be more to the story because not even Drake was that bad at prioritizing.

Thankfully, the conversation took a different course.

"—Triple D?"

"Good, good. We actually just moved into a new place. Come to think of it, that's kinda why I'm here. I wanted to chat with Beckett about a particular case."

"Oh, cool. Well, he's in his office—follow me."

Screech smiled. It took all his willpower not to stick his tongue out at the secretary as he walked past.

Chapter 30

The elevator pinged and the doors to Ken Smith's penthouse condo opened. Drake stepped into the lavish space, breathing in the thick cigar smoke. The back of the mayor's chair was facing him, but he could make out tendrils of smoke rising from the man seated in it.

"Ken," he cursed.

The reply came in the form of a hearty, deep-throated chuckle.

Furious, Drake strode forward, grabbing the back of the chair with both hands. He intended on spinning it around, or in the very least toppling it when a figure rose in front of it.

"Jasmine?" Drake gasped, stumbling backward.

She wiped her lips with the back of her hand as if it weren't clear enough what she'd been doing. Instead of defending herself, or saying anything at all, Jasmine just looked at him, her eyes dark and blank.

The laugh got louder.

When Drake finally came to his senses, he grabbed the back of Ken's chair again and wrenched it around. It spun fluidly enough that Drake had to step back to avoid being struck.

What he saw this time set him off-balance, so much so that he fell on his ass.

Ken Smith was seated in his chair, the pants of his bespoke suit spread wide, a massive Cuban cigar dangling between his fingers.

Only he didn't look the way Drake remembered him. He didn't look like a person at all. This Ken Smith didn't have any skin or blood or sinew to speak of. He was a skeleton.

And cemented atop his gleaming skull was a crown of finger bones.

It was the Skeleton King—he was back.

The chuckle was suddenly so loud that Drake felt that his head might explode. He dropped to the ground and curled into the fetal position, pressing his palms against the sides of his head in an attempt to block out the terrible sound.

It was no use.

The sound wasn't coming from the Skeleton King or from Jasmine or from anywhere in the apartment.

It was coming from him; Drake was the one laughing.

Chapter 31

"DON'T BE SUCH A FUCKING child, Beckett," Suzan said as she opened the door. "He knows you're in here—we both do."

Screech followed Suzan into the office, his eyes darting about the room.

It wasn't a particularly large office with barely enough room to fit a microscope and a computer on the sole desk. But said desk was large enough to hide a full-grown man beneath.

"Beckett, I just—"

"I'm not here," a voice hollered. "Move along now."

Suzan rolled her eyes and shrugged. As she walked around to the other side of the desk, Screech's gaze fell on an open newspaper resting half on and half off the microscope. The main feature was of some sort of pastor or preacher and the man's face was circled in red pen. There were also Xs on his eyes, and someone had drawn a red tongue lolling out of his mouth.

The title read, *Father Alistair Cameron Cures Death.*

Very subtle, Screech thought. *Who was it written by? The Pope?*

"Just get up," Suzan said, her voice dripping with annoyance.

This seemed to do it; Beckett suddenly crawled out from beneath his desk.

"Oh, fancy seeing you guys here. My meeting ended early, soooo…" He ran his hand through his blond hair and shrugged. "Oh, Screech, always a pleasure. What can I do you for?"

Screech sighed. Despite the charade, it was clear that he wasn't the only one dreading this encounter.

"I need a favor."

A mock smile appeared on Beckett's lips.

"Of course you do, shit, I expected nothing less." He turned to Suzan and waved a hand in her direction, not bothering to hide his annoyance at the fact that she'd let Screech into his office. "Move along now, little Suze. The grown-ups need to do a little talky-talky."

Suzan's lips formed an O shape.

"Keep it up, Beckett; you know that vacation you promised me? Well, the number of stars at the hotel we're going to stay at just jumped up as did the price tag. I'm thinking that this is gonna be a Cardi B-style vacation, minus the stripping. What do you think?"

Without waiting for an answer, Suzan turned and left the room. When she was gone, Beckett walked over and made sure that the door was closed. Then he took a seat at his desk and folded his arms across his chest. He was no longer smiling.

"What do you want, Screech? I already told you that I can't be involved with Drake anymore. I just can't do it."

Screech nodded; the man had never been shy about his feelings regarding Drake.

Friends, foes, lovers, hoes… isn't that how the song goes?

Screech tried to clear his head; obviously, he hadn't gotten as much sleep as he thought he had.

"It's not about Drake, it's about a client of mine. A Mrs. Armatridge… apparently, she's been charged with murdering her husband. I managed to get one of my guys, Leroy, to pull the ME report, which was done by a Dr. Karen Nordmeyer? Anyways, it states that the man had been killed, likely by being pushed *up* the stairs."

Becket stared at him blankly.

"And?"

"And I was hoping you could look into it? I mean, the woman spends most of her time in a wheelchair. I don't know if..." Screech let his sentence trail off, hoping that Beckett would cut in with a comment.

He didn't.

"She's an eighty-one-year-old woman, Beckett. And I mean, sure, she has some issues, don't get me wrong, but I doubt she killed her husband. Do you think—"

"Do I think, what? Do I think that I can go and interrogate one of my underlings about a medical report that she wrote on this Mrs. Armatridge? Do I think I should further alienate myself from my peers and my community? For you? For Drake? For Triple D?"

"Actually, we're not called Triple D anymore. We're now—"

"I care not."

Screech chewed the inside of his lip, fighting the urge to plead his case further. He hadn't expected such a visceral reaction from Beckett. Sure, he'd thought that the doctor would be annoyed, but this was different.

This seemed like... like *fear*, if he didn't know any better.

"Screech, how many—" Beckett stopped mid-sentence and grabbed his forehead.

"You okay? Beckett?"

Beckett continued to grimace even as he reached for the top drawer of his desk with his free hand. Screech watched as he popped open a bottle of Aspirin and chewed three different tabs.

"Yeah, fine. I'm fine. Just a headache. See what you've done? You come here, and all of a sudden I have a headache."

"I'm sorry. To be honest, I didn't want to come here. I really didn't. But I need help, and I didn't know where else to turn."

"Why do I get the sneaking suspicion that it isn't just about Mrs. Armadillo's dead husband? Why do I think that there are many more layers to this onion, Screech?"

Screech glanced at his feet in silent admission.

"Yeah, that's what I thought. I'll tell you what, Screech, I will look into this, but if I'm letting you take me from behind, grip my hips and whatnot, you have to do the honorable thing."

Screech's eyes flicked up.

"Excuse me?"

"A reach around; it's only polite."

It took Screech a couple of seconds to understand the meaning behind the man's crude analogy. This was another reason why he'd dreaded coming here. The last thing he wanted was to owe Dr. Becket Campbell a favor.

But what choice did he have?

"Okay," he nearly whispered. "Fine."

"Shout it; I want you to shout my name, Screech. I want you to put your hands in the air and shout my name to the heavens like you mean it."

Screech took a deep breath and started to raise his arms.

"Dr. Beckett Camp—"

"Are you retarded? Keep your voice down, Screech. Jesus." Beckett stood, a smirk appearing on his face. "I'll look into it. How's Drake, anyway?"

Screech swallowed hard.

"He's on vacation," he replied. It wasn't a lie, not completely. But he didn't see any value in telling Beckett that Drake had left his girlfriend and kid to go to Colombia, of all places, to hunt down Ken Smith.

"Damn, I wish he'd taken Suzan with him. This trip really is gonna cost me."

Chapter 32

A FILTHY HAND COVERED DRAKE'S mouth, silencing his scream. His eyes snapped open and he immediately started to struggle. But with his hands still bound behind him, the best he could manage was a languid kick at his assailant.

The hand on his face tightened and a knee was crossed over his shins, stopping his feeble leg thrusts.

This is it, Drake thought absently. *This is how I die: alone and tied up in a filthy dungeon. This is the end.*

And yet, despite this revelation, he didn't feel a sudden pang of sadness that one might expect.

If anything, Drake felt relief.

"Shut up," a familiar voice hissed in his ear. "Stop screaming and keep your voice down."

The man pulled back and Drake finally got a clear look at him.

A single word, first uttered by Diego, echoed in his head.

El phantasmo.

"I'm going to pull my hand away from your mouth, but you can't scream."

The man nodded and slowly released his grip on Drake's face.

"Dane? What the hell are you doing here?"

His brother brought a finger to his lips and hushed him. Then he reached behind Drake's back and snapped the zip tie that bound his hands.

Drake grunted and pulled his hands out in front of him. They'd been bound together for so long, that his shoulders had long since gone numb. And now, as blood flooded his arms again, he fought the urge to cry out once more.

"Can you walk?" his brother asked.

Drake simply stared at the man for a second. His face was covered in some sort of black paint and he was wearing a camo hat and fatigues. In short, Dane Drake looked like a soldier straight out of Apocalypse Now.

Dane reached out and slapped Drake gently across the face.

"Damien, can you walk? We need to get out of here—I don't know how long Wesley will be away."

Drake blinked again but eventually nodded. He needed his brother's help to rise to his feet but after stretching his legs, he found that he could indeed walk.

Together, with his brother's arm wrapped around his waist and the other one leading with a pistol, they made their way to the open cell door.

There were so many questions running through Drake's mind that it almost made him dizzy. And when he saw several men, one of whom was the massive security guard from the medical center, with bullet holes in the backs of their heads, lying flat on their faces, he felt sick.

He knew he shouldn't look, but when they stepped over the bodies, Drake couldn't help himself.

They'd had no chance; none of them had even pulled their weapons.

"Jesus," Drake nearly moaned. When Dane pulled his arm, he looked over at his brother. The man's face was a thin pink line buried in the war paint.

He seemed unfazed by the carnage that he'd inflicted.

For some reason, Beckett's words came to him then: *Everything you touch, every person you come in contact with, turns to shit. You try to do good, to do the right thing, but everything always seems to turn so wrong.*

Sure, these men had kidnapped him and, if Wesley was to be believed, would have killed him without a second thought.

But if it weren't for him, if Drake wasn't here, if he hadn't smuggled himself into the country, these men would still be alive. And who's to say that Wesley or Ken didn't hold something over them to get them to do their bidding like they had with Diego?

Did they really deserve to be gunned down like cattle in an unregulated abattoir?

Bile suddenly rose in his throat and his stomach lurched. Sensing this change, his brother looked at him, then yanked his arm. Drake stumbled through a dark passage, his swollen head and confused mind barely taking in the fact that they were deep underground somewhere.

He became disoriented, and if it weren't for Dane pulling him along, Drake had no doubt that he would have quickly become lost. Eventually, they climbed up a small ladder and emerged in a diner of sorts.

The smell of grease and fried food only worsened his nausea and when they passed over two more dead bodies, one of whom was still wearing an apron, Drake started to lose the battle with his roiling guts.

Dane was unrelenting, pulling Drake through the doors and into the night.

No sooner had his heels hit the sidewalk, however, did Drake drive them down.

Then he buckled over at the waist and vomited. Three bouts later, he wiped his mouth and lifted his eyes.

Dane stared back. With only the moonlight illuminating him from behind, he really did look like a *phantasmo*.

"We have to go," he said, pointing to a rusted pickup that was idling by the curb. There was a driver inside and he was gesturing madly out the window at them. "Damien, we need to go, *now!*"

Chapter 33

"THIS IS BULLSHIT," SCREECH GRUMBLED as he struggled to adjust his shirt. No matter what he did, it kept riding up and ruffling about his middle, making him look fat. "These damn shirts have all these buttons, but no one thought to put buttons on the bottom so that you can fasten to your pants, so it never moves up?"

Hanna looked over at him and laughed.

"You look… you look like a used Bible salesman."

Screech growled.

"Not much of a fucking market for those, is there?".

Hanna laughed again. She was wearing a dark blouse and fitted jeans, complete with thick heels. She looked pretty good, actually. Good and *comfortable*.

"Yeah, I'd go easy on the Bible jokes," Leroy warned from the back seat.

"Oh, great," Hanna complained. "Why did you have to say that? Now I'll be thinking about Bible jokes all night."

Screech glared at her.

"What?"

"A while back, I was dating this guy from Russia and one time he told me that his sister was planning a visit from the motherland. He asked if I wanted to meet her, and I said sure. Everything was fine leading up to the encounter, but when we were in a cab going to meet her at a restaurant, he leans over to me and says, 'you know, my sister has a good sense of humor, but it's probably best to lay off the land mine jokes.' I was like, what the hell? I didn't even think I knew any land mine jokes. But, sure enough, I knew *one*. And, within ten minutes of meeting Mina, I just blurted it out. If he hadn't warned me, I would have never said a stupid land mine joke, but because he did, it was like impossible not to!"

Screech made a face.

"There's something wrong with you."

Hanna laughed.

"Sure, but let me ask you this: how did Moses make his coffee?"

"Hanna, seriously, what the hell is wrong with you?"

"Hebrews it."

Screech shook his head and Leroy groaned.

"Yeah, don't say I didn't warn you." The boy fingered the chain that had once belonged to his brother but was now buried beneath his T-shirt as he spoke.

Eager to change the subject, Screech said, "Hey, how come you get to wear a T-shirt, but I gotta wear this god—uhh, this stupid dress shirt?"

"Because you're the boss, that's why. Look, unless you want DSLH Investigations to become DSH Investigations, you're gonna have to act all professional-like."

"DSH Investigations," Screech grumbled as he tried once more to adjust his shirt. "Fewer mouths to feed."

"Be nice now, Screech," Hanna said, using her best motherly voice.

Screech's scowl deepened.

"Hanna, I'm going to get you back for this. When—"

"There it is," Leroy said, pointing at an apartment complex to their right.

Uncomfortable as he felt, Screech was also proud of what he'd done; when Leroy had told him the whole story of what happened to his brother, and then to his mom—how she'd been assaulted in her own apartment—he'd had no problem giving the man an advance on his first check.

He figured he owed him anyway, given that they'd nearly been mowed down by a maniac with a machine gun. And now, seeing the modest but safe digs that the boy's mother had moved into, he felt good.

After all the things he'd done with Drake over the years that made him feel dirty, this made him actually feel *good*. And that was worth the cash he'd shelled out.

Screech parked the car and was stepping out of the vehicle when his shirt came untucked again.

"Jesus Christ," he grumbled, jamming it back into his pants.

"Now, now, Screechie-poo," Hanna mocked.

Screech tucked the bottle of wine under one arm then reached out to swat her. He missed, but she got the idea and didn't say anything else until they got to the door.

***

"Hi, Mom," Leroy said, as he leaned into the apartment and gave his mother a kiss.

"Leroy," the woman replied curtly.

Kinesha Walker was a tall, thin woman with her hair pulled back in cornrows. She was attractive, which wasn't surprising given the fact that Leroy himself was a good-looking young man.

But what Screech hadn't been prepared for were the laser beams coming out of her eyeballs, aimed directly at him.

The stare made him even more uncomfortable than his shirt.

"Hi, my name is Screech—uhh, I mean Stephen. Stephen Thompson," he blubbered, holding the wine out to her.

Kinesha glanced down at the bottle but didn't take it.

"This is a dry household, Screech Stephen," she said, pressing her full lips together.

Screech's face went beet red. Hanna scoffed, and he thrust an elbow in her direction. She deftly dodged the blow and stepped forward, extending her hand.

"My name's Hanna," she said softly. "It's a pleasure to meet you."

"I've heard a lot about you, Hanna," Kinesha replied as they shook hands. "Leroy speaks very highly of you."

What the fuck? What did I do wrong?

"Come on in and make yourself comfortable," she said, gesturing to the interior of the apartment. "I've got something I need to tend to on the stove."

Leroy stepped inside, and Hanna followed.

Screech looked at the wine bottle in his hand, debating whether he should leave it outside the door or bring it inside with him.

In the end, he decided to bring it along.

"You could've told me about the wine," Screech whispered in Leroy's ear as he removed his shoes.

Leroy looked over at Hanna and winked.

"What would be the fun in that?"

Screech scowled and was about to condemn the boy when his shirt came untucked again.

Chapter 34

IT WAS JUST DRAKE AND Dane now. The Colombian man who had driven them to the remote location had left shortly after dropping them off. Not before exchanging words with Dane, however, words uttered too quietly for Drake to hear.

But Drake didn't care. He didn't even care that all they had between them was a bag of basic supplies and a couple of dull machetes. He didn't even care that all he had to fill his stomach was extra-salty jerky and a warm beer.

What he cared about was all those dead people back in the diner and in the dungeon beneath.

Sure, he'd killed people before; he'd killed many of them on his way to saving Mandy and Veronica. But that had been different. These people... these Colombians had been killed because somebody was trying to save *him*. And he wasn't worth saving.

"What happened to you, Dane?" he asked softly between chews of the tough jerky.

When his brother looked at him quizzically, he realized that it was much too broad a question. So, he clarified.

"What happened to you on the boat?"

Dane swallowed some beer and then answered the question in his flat affect that Drake was becoming accustomed to.

"Wesley tried to take me out," he replied. "But I knew it was going to happen and I got the jump on him. The bastard got away, though. Set the whole goddamn boat on fire."

Drake made no effort to hide his unease.

"Why were you even on the boat in the first place?"

This time, Dane refused to answer and simply shook his head. They continued to munch on beef jerky and take swallows of warm beer for the next several minutes in silence.

Drake wasn't sure what time it was, but it was clear that the harsh blanket of night would lift in a few hours. Where they would go next, however, was less certain.

"How did you know where to find me?"

"You stand out like a sore thumb. Ken and Wesley might have most of the local drug trade working for them, but I still have a few loyal men. Like Pablo who drove us out here."

Out here...

Drake looked around. He was reminded of when he'd just stepped off the boat and onto Colombian soil. They were surrounded by lush, green vegetation devoid of landmarks.

"And where, exactly, are we?

"Colombia," Dane replied. Drake's first thought was that his brother was making a joke. But looking at that face... he got the impression that Dane didn't have much of a sense of humor. At least, not anymore.

It was a simple, almost childish answer but, in a way, it was also a satisfactory one. The truth was, it didn't really matter where they were, all that mattered to Drake, all that *ever* mattered, was that Ken and now Wesley Smith were here, too. And while he was grateful that his brother was alive and that he'd saved Drake's life, he still had a job to do.

And Drake was nothing if not determined.

Dane tossed his empty beer bottle over his shoulder then reached into his bag. He pulled out a pair of fatigues and a heavy sweatshirt.

"Put these on. It gets cool in the early morning hours. And then see if you can get some sleep; we've got a long day of hiking tomorrow."

Chapter 35

"SO, DID YOU FINISH COLLEGE, Stephen?" Kinesha asked from across the table.

Screech hard-swallowed the chicken that he'd been chewing.

"No, I didn't finish it. I went for a few years — computer sciences — but I didn't finish my degree."

He didn't know why he felt guilty admitting this; after all, he'd come to terms with this long ago, as had his parents — they were just glad that he wasn't in and out of prison like his brother — but he did.

He felt guilty and ashamed.

This woman, this Kinesha Walker... she was so intimidating that it was like she was Screech's mom and not Leroy's.

"What about you, Hanna?"

Hanna nodded, took a sip of her iced tea, and then said, "I did my undergrad in psychology, and then completed a master's degree in human behavior."

Screech was glad that he'd already swallowed his chicken; if he hadn't, it might have fallen right out of his mouth and onto his plate.

A Master's degree? Who the fuck is this person?

Even Leroy, who had been an even keel all dinner, seemed taken aback by this.

"I just love learning about how people behave, about the underlying reasons for their actions."

Kinesha was beaming now and if Hanna had been across from him, Screech might have kicked her under the table. He didn't know if what she was saying was true, but it seemed that everything that came out of her mouth just made him look like a larger pile of garbage.

A hot, steaming pile of garbage.

"Yeah, I also find people's behavior and actions interesting," Kinesha said, her eyes on Screech the entire time as if admonishing his own actions.

What in the Sam hell did I do wrong here?

"The chicken is delicious as usual, Mom," Leroy said when there was a lull in the conversation.

"It's *very* good," Screech added. He cringed at his own words; he felt like a teenager on a first date trying to impress the woman's father. Only, in this case, Leroy was his date and it was his mother who was giving him fits.

"Thank you," she said, rising from the table.

"Please, sit," Hanna interjected. "I'll clean."

"Why thank you, Hanna."

Kinesha smiled and sat back down again. Hanna promptly took hers and Leroy's plates into the kitchen.

What a kiss ass.

While Hanna was out of the room, Kinesha turned her focus back to Screech.

"Stephen, where's the other man that Leroy is always talking about? Where's Drake?"

Screech looked over at Leroy accusingly. He had no idea that the man's mother knew about Drake.

"He, uhh, well, he's taking a little time off, a little break. But I assure you, Drake—"

"So, you're the one in charge, then?"

"Well, we're a team, really. I mean—"

"My son is barely eighteen years old… you mean to tell me that he's in charge? That…"

Hanna reappeared to collect Screech's plate. Her timing was impeccable and therefore likely planned.

"What Stephen means to say, is that we work through everything together—discuss all our clients. But when it comes to the big decisions, yes, Stephen is the one who has the final say."

"I see."

"And is there any danger involved in your business? I mean, I appreciate what you've done for Leroy and our living situation, but the last thing I want is for him to be in danger."

Screech pictured Leroy first at the trap house trying to sell the thugs' own heroin back to them and then in the back of the police cruiser, a gun aimed between his eyes.

"No, of course not. Most of the time, we're just following up with old ladies who misplaced their silverware." *Not a lie, really.* "But I appreciate your concern. To be honest, Leroy is mostly a behind-the-scenes guy, until he gets his feet wet. He's just going to be helping me with the computers, doing background research, that sort of thing."

Leroy smiled and pulled something out of his pocket.

"Check this out, Mom, I got my own PI badge."

He handed the badge to his mom who gave it a cursory glance, before placing it down on the table.

"He *will* be finishing high school. I also want him to go to college."

Another hard swallow.

"If Leroy wants to go to college, he can go to college. I have no problem with that."

Kinesha nodded curtly.

"And benefits? What are the health and dental benefits like at DH-whatever Investigations?"

Screech was over his head, and everyone at the table knew it, or so he thought. Just a few months ago it only had been him and Drake, and Drake didn't really give a shit what happened with the business provided he got his man. Now, ever since bringing Hanna and Leroy on board, things had become complicated.

"Stephen? What about benefits?"

Hanna returned from the kitchen.

"Yeah, Stephen, I'm expecting that DSLH will have full health and dental benefits? Because, you know, those things are expensive. I'm also thinking about maternity leave." She turned to Kinesha. "Not now, of course, but in the future."

Oh, shit, why not throw in free flights around the world while I'm at it?

Screech realized that he was scowling, and he tried to smile as he faced Kinesha.

"I'm still working out the details, but I'm pretty sure that we'll have full health and dental at DSLH."

"Pretty sure"

This is ridiculous.

"Yes," he barely croaked. "Full dental and health."

Kinesha was beaming now.

"Great, just great. Well, provided Leroy stays in school and finishes, I suppose that I can approve of this."

"Awesome," Screech said glumly. "Now, what's for dessert?"

Chapter 36

DRAKE BARELY SLEPT AT ALL during what was left of the night. This was partly because he was sore all over, he had a headache, his liver hurt, his wrists ached, but mostly because he was afraid to dream.

For as long as he could remember, he dreamed about Clay and what happened that night. But after the man responsible—Ray Reynolds—had committed suicide with the rest of his congregation, the nightmares had faded.

But now, the Skeleton King had returned, this time wearing Ken Smith's expensive threads. And then there was Jasmine. Jasmine was entrenched in this whole mess, somehow involved with the heroin ring. He had no idea how or why, but the photo he'd left on her doorstep was evidence enough for him.

After this was all over, if he managed to take care of Ken and Wesley and make it out of Colombia alive, Drake wondered if he would ever be able to see his son again. Then he questioned if that would be a good idea, for either of them.

After all, Beckett was right. Everything he touched turned to shit.

He didn't know why, but that was just his fate.

The sunrise in the jungle that morning was one of the most beautiful things he'd ever seen. Light filtered down through the dew-covered trees, forming rainbows everywhere he looked. The jungle itself slowly came alive, as well, first with the sound of birds, and then with insects chasing the last vestiges of night away.

With the sun came the heat, and Drake took off the sweatshirt his brother had given him. He located the bag that they'd pulled their paltry meal out of the night before, and he stood with the intention of putting the sweatshirt in it. Drake stopped when he realized that his brother was also awake and that he was staring at him. Most of the war paint had worn off and, in the early morning light, Dane looked less commando and more his brother.

"What happened to you?" Drake asked instinctively. He expected his brother to ignore the question, but the man tossed him some beef jerky and then nodded.

For some reason, even though the night before this very question had been too broad, too ambiguous, it was more poignant now, and Dane knew exactly what he was referring to. And, to Drake's surprise, he also answered.

"Suffering," Dane said simply. He indicated the cutlass standing upright in the soil and Drake picked it up. It was surprisingly heavy, and the handle well worn. Dane gripped a nearly identical one in his own hand. "I witnessed suffering, Drake. That's what happened to me. I was too young to see the things Ray Reynolds did to his parents. It changed me. And then when I came here, I saw more things, horrible things. After that, there was no going back."

Dane's candidness was shocking, and Drake didn't dare interrupt. The man slung his bag over one shoulder and then started toward the treeline, swinging his cutlass pre-emptively.

"I knew about life and death, of course; I wasn't a child," he continued. "But I saw things… I saw such *suffering*. Ray only knew how to deal with it one way, and I saw that, too."

His brother delivered a particularly savage swipe to an outcropping of ferns and Drake got the idea, loud and clear. And he understood, in a way; after all, he'd been a shell of his former self ever since the day Clay had been murdered.

"I came here, to South America. Started living off the land, all that shit. Traveling. Trying to clear my head, to find somewhere in this world that wasn't *suffering*. But that place just doesn't exist. I met people along the way, people with connections back in New York. Powerful people, people who—"

"Ken Smith."

Drake couldn't help himself this time. He came up next to his brother and started hacking at the foliage as the jungle became denser.

"People who knew him, people like him, anyway," Dane confirmed. "People like me."

The comment took Drake by surprise. His brother wasn't like Ken Smith, he wasn't like Raul, and he wasn't like Wesley Smith.

His brother was a good man. Twice, Dane had saved his life now. Once at Ray Reynolds's farm when Drake had almost taken his own life, and then here in Colombia.

His brother wasn't an uncaring, megalomaniac seeking power above all else.

For fuck's sake, he was his *brother*.

Images of the dead bodies in the diner threatened to break this impression, but Drake forced them away.

"Where we going, Dane?" he asked, changing the subject.

Dane gripped his cutlass even tighter as he turned to look at him.

"We're going to put an end to this, Drake. We're going to put an end to this suffering once and for all."

Chapter 37

"NOPE," HANNA SAID, CROSSING HER arms defiantly. "No fucking way in heaven or hell am I wearing that."

Screech smirked, thinking about how she'd thrown him under the bus the night before at Leroy's dinner.

"You have to—you *have* to wear the dress. It's the only way you're gonna get into this."

Hanna took the dress, which was a step in the right direction, and held it at arm's length. It was pink, it had lace, and it had poof. *Plenty* of poof.

Leroy guffawed.

"It looks like a fucking debutante ball dress, Screech. She looks like a woman being auctioned off to her uncle!"

That was it. The stress combined with the ridiculous imagery pushed Screech over the edge.

He burst out laughing.

In fact, Screech laughed so hard that he actually bent at the waist.

"You got a tiara for me to wear, as well?"

Hanna's question made Screech collapse to the floor. His laughter had become so debilitating that he could barely reach into the bag that the dress had come in. After watching this for a few moments, Hanna, still scowling, snatched the bag from him and reached inside.

"You've gotta be fucking kidding me."

She took the tiara out and launched it across the room.

Leroy was in stitches now as well, hollering and slapping at his thighs.

The fact that Hanna was standing there watching them, stone-faced, arms crossed over her chest, only made Screech laugh harder. It took a good five whole minutes for the two of them to stop laughing, and another minute to catch their breath.

"I can't believe I agreed to this."

And yet, Screech could tell that she was going to be a good sport about it.

"You have to."

"Fuck... okay, okay, but I'm making some modifications. I'm getting rid of this lace and some of the damn poofy shit."

Screech shook his head and wiped tears from his eyes.

"That thing cost me five-hundred bucks. You can't cut it, because I have to take it back after the *bawl*."

Hanna grinned.

"In that case, you can count on me spilling some red wine on it, teriyaki sauce, maybe."

"Then it's coming out of your paycheck," Screech said, still smiling.

"That's all right, I'll just cash in my full dental work coverage. I was thinking about getting all my teeth replaced by big metal fuckers like the guy from 007."

Screech stopped laughing.

"Yeah, and I think I'll get braces," Leroy chimed in.

"To hell, you will."

After things calmed down, and they'd gotten the giggles out of their system, the trio got to work.

"So, basically, we just want to get in there, set up some cameras, get some eyes on Steffani Loomis, if you can. You'll be wired for sound with an earpiece and I've got a bunch of button cameras that you can place around the estate if things go according to plan. There's also this pendant that you're gonna wear, which will also take video," Screech informed Hanna. "I don't know what we're going to catch on video, if anything, but we're going to try. The key here is that we just want to look. Be polite, nod, curtsy, whatever, but don't engage these people more than you have to."

Hanna nodded.

"Aye, aye Captain, look but no touchy, touchy — strip club rules, only."

"Yeah, something like that."

"So, you're the tech guy and I'm the spy… does that make Leroy the ammunitions guy?" Hanna asked, looking over at the kid.

Leroy made a face.

"Why? Because I'm black?"

Hanna looked around dramatically.

"Because you're the only other person here, dumbass. And if we're going to pose as some sort of retarded A-Team, we *need* an ammunitions guy. Okay, B.A. Baracus?"

"He's not an ammunitions guy," Screech said, rolling his eyes. "You heard his mom, we can't put him in any sort of dangerous situation. She'll murder us. Besides, he's the only one *not* licensed to carry a gun here."

"Speaking of which," Hanna interrupted, "Lots of poof up in this dress, lots of places to hide some guns."

Screech shook his head.

"No, no way. You're not carrying any weapon in there. Strip club rules, remember?"

Hanna made a face but nodded.

"So, if I'm not the ammunitions guy, what the hell am I going to do?" Leroy asked.

"Oh, you've got a pretty important job," Screech said, spinning his computer monitor around.

Leroy squinted at the image of an elderly black man.

"What the — who the hell is this?"

"That's you," Screech said with a grin. "At least, that's who you're *going* to be after you borrow his security badge."

Leroy balked.

"You've gotta be kidding me. I thought you were racist before when you suggested that I'm the weapons guy, but now you want me to be the Butler? And he's eighty for Christ's sake!"

Hanna couldn't help but chuckle.

"Hey, we've all got a role to play here," she said. "I'm sure it'll be fun."

"I wouldn't laugh too hard, Hanna," Screech said, glancing down at his watch. "Because I think it's about time you spoke to your fairy godmother and got into your prom dress, *sweetheart*."

PART III

The Princess of the Ball

Chapter 38

DR. BECKETT CAMPBELL, SENIOR MEDICAL Examiner for the state of New York, walked with purpose down the hallway. He'd already confirmed that the body of Mr. Armand Armatridge was being housed in a cold room at the New York State Morgue. He'd read the file and had gone ahead and let the Medical Examiner who had signed off on the body—a Dr. Karen Nordmeyer—know that he was going to take another look.

And if her tone on the phone was any indication, culminated by the fact that she'd insisted on being present, Beckett figured that Dr. Nordmeyer was none too pleased about this development.

Professional courtesy decreed that you didn't undermine or challenge a fellow colleague's final report, unless it was court mandated, of course. Even then, you tried your best to split hairs and parse infinitives to make sure that everyone understood that any inherent differences were a matter of opinion and not medicine.

Yeah, right.

Beckett loathed these "unwritten" rules, but the idea of someone reviewing and challenging his own work… well, that simply wouldn't be acceptable.

He was surprised to see Dr. Nordmeyer waiting for him in the cold room that housed Armand Armatridge's body. She was a mousy woman, short, a little stocky, and with her arms crossed over her chest the way they were now, she looked like a little ball of hate.

"Dr. Nordmeyer," Beckett said, feigning joviality. He went so far as to reach out to hug the woman—anything to make her even more uncomfortable—but she recoiled as if he were some sort of leper.

And, in the medical community, he supposed that he was. Minus the contagious part.

"I'd ask you again why you're looking into this case," she said. "But I know you wouldn't tell me."

Beckett grinned.

"The perks of being the boss, I guess."

"More like the perks of being an asshole," she whispered under her breath.

Beckett let this go; he'd been called worse, by Suzan no less, and the truth was, he was a bit of an asshole.

He shook his head.

No, that wasn't right; he wasn't a 'bit of an asshole' but a giant, wizard's sleeve of an asshole.

But a snowflake, he was not.

Beckett hooked a chin at the body locker that Dr. Nordmeyer stood defiantly in front of.

"This is where our friend Armand is napping?"

Dr. Nordmeyer scowled and stepped aside.

It was as good as a, 'yes sir, thank you, sir.'

Beckett pulled the door open, then reached for the handle on the tray inside. As he slid the body out, Dr. Nordmeyer spoke up again.

"Is there some reason why you're doing this to me?"

With the tray halfway out, Beckett turned to the woman.

"To *you*? You millennials… everything is always about you, isn't it? Why can't it just be about getting it right?"

Dr. Nordmeyer's lips twisted into a sinister smile that he didn't care for.

"You really don't remember this case, do you?"

This threw Beckett for a loop, and he hesitated, racking his brain to figure out if she was just making shit up.

"No, I guess I don't," he admitted at last.

Nordmeyer scoffed.

"I came to you asking for help on this one, for your opinion—no, wait, *you* came to me, *offering* your opinion. Dr. Campbell, *you're* the one who said that Armand had been pushed *up* the stairs."

Beckett squinted at the woman. He felt the beginnings of another headache coming on, despite the three Aspirin he'd popped this morning.

They were getting worse and more frequent.

"Shoved *up* the stairs?"

None of this rang a bell. He thought that there was a hint of a memory of meeting this woman, this Dr. Karen Nordmeyer before, but that was around the time that he was dealing with the McEwing girl. The time when he was adding to his tattoo collection.

A strange tingling started in his fingertips then, almost as if it was a symptom of his burgeoning headache.

A tingling, an urge.

Beckett realized that Dr. Nordmeyer was speaking to him—her lips were moving—but he wasn't hearing any words. For some strange reason, he was fixated on the inner corner of her right eye. He simply couldn't look away from her tear duct. The tingling intensified, and he envisioned himself taking a pencil out of his pocket, pulling the woman's head back, and jamming the sharpened tip into the tear duct.

A sudden flash of pain shot from temple to temple and he winced.

"Are you even listening to me?"

Beckett shook his head and his headache subsided.

"You were saying something about this stiff. Something about me signing off on him?" The phrase came out as more of a question than a statement, and the look of confusion that washed over Dr. Nordmeyer's face confirmed that she'd long since moved on from this point.

"You came into this very room and told me that there were bruises on the man's back from where he was pushed. Remember? The man's wife claimed that she was outside at the time of his fall. He was in a wheelchair at the time. You really don't remember this? It was less than a month ago."

Beckett blinked twice and some of the memory started coming back to him. He recalled rolling the man's body over and looking at bruises on his back.

"There are these strange gouges in his head, deep gouges, but no blunt force trauma." As the doctor rambled on, Beckett slid the tray all the way out and then stared at the white sheet that covered Mr. Armatridge's body. "You said that he probably fell up the stairs, but that he'd been shoved."

Beckett slowly teased the sheet back and stared down at the man's pale face. He offered a cursory glance at the wounds in his head, and more of the memory of seeing him before came flooding back. There were seven gashes on his chrome dome, three of which were longer and deeper than the others. Reserving closer inspection of these wounds for later, he spent a few moments inspecting his legs. They weren't the atrophy limbs of a man who couldn't walk. Make no mistake, Mr. Armatridge was no quadzilla either, but it was clear that this man, while he might've been wheelchair-bound for most of the day, still had use of his legs.

Just like Mrs. Armatridge, if Screech was to be believed.

"If you change my final report, if you overrule what I wrote, the police are going to ask questions—the wife has already been charged. And if that happens, they'll go to the board. Is that what you want?"

Once again, Beckett ignored her as he continued to scan the body. The bruising on his back was more obvious now that the body was nearly as white as the sheet that had covered it. And these marks really did look like hand prints. But how strong would you have to be to leave them, was the real question.

"Do you want this department to be scrutinized after all that—"

"I'm sorry," Beckett said, raising his eyes and offering a placating smile. "Are you still speaking? I mean, your lips are moving, but no intelligible sounds are coming out."

Dr. Nordmeyer glared at him.

"Why don't you make yourself useful and go fetch me a photograph of the man's wheelchair, would you, please?"

Chapter 39

LEROY VAULTED HIMSELF OVER THE short wrought iron fence. As soon as his sneakers hit the grass, he took off running, trying his best to stay out of the bright lights that illuminated the yard. He made it across the lawn without being noticed, then pressed his back up against the brick wall. He paused to catch his breath and to try to slow his rapidly beating heart.

Mom said to get out, he thought with a touch of disdain. *I guess this qualifies.*

For the first time since starting at DSLH, Leroy considered that taking her advice about going to college might have been the smarter choice. Instead, he found himself here, in the process of breaking half a dozen laws and subjecting him to further scrutiny by the morally-inept New York elite.

Buck up, Leroy. These people were responsible for your brother's death. There is no better way to honor him than to make sure they get what's comin'.

Leroy craned his neck around the corner and immediately spotted a man with his back to him, wearing an identical white shirt and black trousers. As he watched, a thick cloud of smoke nearly engulfed the man's head.

One final deep breath and Leroy smoothed his shirt and stepped out into the open.

"Excuse me," he said, as he made his way toward the man.

When he didn't turn, Leroy raised his voice.

"Excuse me?"

The man turned, and his lined face suddenly went flaccid. Leroy watched as he slipped the hand holding the joint down to his hip before dropping it to the grass. Then he slid his heel over top of it to stamp it out.

None of these were half as subtle as the man thought they were.

"I was just, uh, I was..."

"Smoking a J," Leroy finished for him. He took several steps forward, and then his own face went slack. "Shit."

In person, the man looked less like him than even in the photo that Screech had pulled up on the computer. Sure, they were both black, but Leroy was a tall and thin eighteen-year-old. This man must have been close to forty, with flecks of gray in his short beard and eyes that were slightly yellowed from years of alcohol abuse.

Fucking Screech, Leroy thought glumly. *We all look the same to you, is that right?*

"Who are you?" the man asked, his tone becoming defensive.

"I'm your replacement," Leroy replied, mustering up as much courage as he could.

The man's eyes narrowed.

"Nuh-uh, I'm here all night. I'm doin' the front door, the checklist."

Leroy shook his head.

"You *were* doing the front door, but now you're going home for the night."

The man's flaccid expression became a scowl and he puffed up his chest a little. He had a good twenty pounds on Leroy and while it was obvious that he'd put his body through the wringer over the years, Leroy wasn't much of a fighter, himself.

And he had no intention of becoming one anytime soon.

"I don't think so."

"Well, okay, let me just, uhh, make a call to your employer, let 'em know that you got high before the charity ball. How 'bout that?"

"It's your word against mine," the man said, but it was clear by the way he leaned back slightly as he spoke that he needed this job, that he wasn't going to risk losing it over a single joint.

Leroy reached slowly and deliberately into his pocket. The man across from him tensed, but then relaxed when he saw the envelope.

Leroy held it out to the man.

"What's this?"

"Just take it," Leroy instructed, shaking it. As he did, the flap, which was intentionally unsealed, flipped up, revealing a wad of bills inside.

"What's this?" he asked again but grabbed the envelope without waiting for an answer.

"Consider this your payment for the night. Of course, you can have your job back tomorrow—no one needs to know. You just have to give me your badge and guest list, is all."

The man scratched his head as he thought this over. Then he glanced down at the heel of his shoe, which was only half-covering the joint that he'd dropped.

"Fuck it, just don't cause no problems," he said, and then promptly handed over his name tag and checklist. "I need this job."

Leroy nodded and watched the man go, counting the cash as he went. When he was alone, he turned his attention to the image on the badge.

He shook his head.

"Looks nothing like me," he muttered.

But in the back of his mind, he knew that Screech was probably right, that this wouldn't matter. With all the rampant racism going around, one of the rich white guests would have to have some serious balls to call him out on it.

Leroy rolled his eyes when he saw what the man's name was.

"C.J. Yobooty? You've gotta be shittin' me."

With a sigh, he clipped the name tag to his shirt. As he did, the tiny covert earpiece crackled to life.

"Hey, C.J., you there?" Screech asked.

Fuck, he knew this guy's name all along!

With a scowl, Leroy dipped his chin to his collar.

"Yeah, I'm here. Got the damn ID and guest list."

"Don't talk into your collar, your voice is picked up by the earpiece as well. Just look natural."

Eyes wide, Leroy looked around but didn't see anyone.

"What? How did you—"

"Don't worry, I'm still back at the office," Screech answered as if reading his mind. "I just figured you'd seen too many spy shows. Just speak and act naturally."

Leroy took a deep breath.

"Okay, fine."

"Good, now collect yourself and get Yobooty to the front door before the guests start to arrive."

Chapter 40

DRAKE WIPED THE SWEAT FROM his brow and took a deep breath. They'd been trudging through the Colombian jungle for nearly six hours now and he was exhausted.

Dane, on the other hand, was relentless, swinging his cutlass in the same wide, shifting arc, in a way that was almost robotic in nature. He truly was a different man than Drake remembered. He'd changed after that summer at the Reynolds's farm, but he'd become a shell after Ray had killed himself.

The worst thing about this revelation was that Drake could see parts of himself in Dane.

Parts he didn't care for.

If it weren't for the fact that his brother would periodically check their coordinates on a handheld GPS device, Drake might have concluded that they were just aimlessly traipsing through the jungle.

It wasn't as if he was forthcoming with information; Dane's cryptic 'we're going to end this' was all he'd offered in terms of directions and was unwilling to expound.

In fact, aside from the few minutes of humanity expressed by his brother that morning, silence had been the rule for the day. For Drake, however, silence had never been quiet; his thoughts were a chorus of screams in his brain.

Which, he knew, was why he drank the way he did. But out here in the jungle, having long since finished the handful of warm beers that Dane had procured from the diner, thinking was all he could do.

And he detested every minute of it.

Ghostly—*phantasmo*—images of Ken, Raul, Wesley, and Clay filled his mind. Occasionally, Jasmine's smiling face would also appear.

"We're here," his brother whispered, pulling Drake out of his head.

He looked around, confusion setting in. There was some sort of hut, right there, not twenty paces from where he stood. A hut, in the center of the jungle.

Drake had to rub his eyes to make sure that this wasn't an exhaustion-fueled mirage.

"Wh—"

Dane turned to him and brought the cutlass to his pursed lips, hushing him. Swallowing hard, Drake hurried up to his brother's side and leaned in close.

"Where are we? Who lives here?"

As he spoke, Drake observed the hut, which was about the size of a large shed and made up of a patchwork of tree trunks and thick leaves and vines.

Dane ignored him and looked down at his GPS device and nodded to himself.

"Dane, what the fuck is going on? Where are we?" Drake pressed.

Dane finally turned to him with red-rimmed eyes. He lowered the cutlass from his face, but his grip on the handle tightened.

"Wait here."

"What?" Drake hissed.

Dane was off, and Drake just missed grabbing the back of his sweat-soaked T-shirt. He moved quickly for a big man, heading not toward the front of the hut, but around the side, sticking close to the thicker vegetation. And then he was gone.

El phantasmo.

Drake ground his teeth in frustration. He was too tired and too sober for this.

Maybe I should just go back, he thought suddenly. *Maybe I should just forget about all this and go back to Jasmine, to Clay.*

He got as far as to look behind him before realizing how foolish this idea was. There was no *back*; there was only the jungle. He was surrounded with no way of getting out. Even if he could find his way back to New York, avoided jail time, and patched things up with Jasmine, it wouldn't be long before the dreams returned.

Dreams of the Skeleton King.

Drake took several deep breaths before jabbing the end of his cutlass into the soft earth. He dropped to one knee and rested his elbow on the handle. As he rested, the entire jungle seemed to go silent and every subsequent blink seemed to last longer than the previous.

Just before sleep took hold, a commotion drew Drake's chin from his chest.

The door to the hut flew open and a man with greasy black hair was shoved onto the grass. He stumbled and then fell on his stomach. When he lifted his head, Drake saw dual streams of blood running from a nose that was no longer true.

"Is this the man?" Dane demanded as he stepped forward aggressively. The sun glinted off his cutlass as he held it high in the air. "Drake, is this the man who gave you up? The man from the boat?"

Drake shook his head.

Man from the boat? What is he talking about?

"Please," the man lying on his stomach whimpered.

Drake's eyes suddenly went wide. Despite the blood and snot and tears coating his face, he recognized the man.

"Diego," Drake almost whispered. His brother nodded and stepped forward.

And then, to Drake's horror, he swung his cutlass down in a looping arc.

"No!" Drake shouted, holding his hand out in front of him.

It was too late; the glinting steel met first flesh, then bone before Drake could do anything about it.

Chapter 41

BECKETT'S EYES MOVED FROM THE photograph of the wheelchair to Mr. Armatridge's bruises, then back again.

Needing a better look, he slid his hands under the man's body and attempted to turn him over. He was heavier than he looked, and Beckett considered asking Dr. Nordmeyer for help. But, seeing the sour expression on her face as she hovered behind him, Beckett decided to save his breath. With a grunt, he managed to flip Mr. Armatridge onto his side, giving him a clear view of the bruises.

Then he looked back at the wheelchair.

The back of the seat had a curious design: there were two oval pads right in the area that Mr. Armatridge had his bruises. There was also a space down the middle of both. Beckett considered that if the man had fallen backward in his chair hard enough, the bruising might have come from these molded pads instead of from a set of hands.

Satisfied that staring at the man's pale back would provide no further insight, Beckett laid him flat again and turned his attention to the wounds that had killed him: the deep gashes in his scalp. His first instinct was that, based on their rounded shape, they were consistent with striking the stairs.

Beckett looked at the crime scene photos next. The thing that didn't jive was the sheer volume of blood in the stairwell. Based on the spray pattern and the collection on the bottom steps, he could see why he'd told Dr. Nordmeyer that it appeared that Mr. Armatridge had been pushed and essentially fallen *up* the stairs.

With a heavy sigh, he picked up a photograph in each hand: one of the wheelchair and one of the stairwell.

Although nothing screamed to him that his initial assessment was categorically wrong, there was something off about the images. While this oddity, whatever it was, might have been ignored by another Medical Examiner—*ahem, Dr. Nordmeyer*—Beckett just simply couldn't turn a blind eye.

Beckett sucked his teeth. According to the police report, Mrs. Armatridge had wheeled herself inside and found her husband lying on the floor in the stairwell. But given the fact that he too was wheelchair-bound, it made sense that he would bring his chair to the bottom step before hoisting himself up. But the crime scene photograph of the chair was *not* in the stairwell, but near the kitchen. It made sense; to get to Mr. Armatridge, his wife would have had to move the chair.

In order to put things back the way they'd been, Beckett reached for a set of scissors.

"Uh, you can't, uh, you can't cut those. They're from the crime scene."

"Print another," Beckett grumbled as he started snipping away. It didn't end up being the greatest cut job—he was a pathologist, not a surgeon, not to mention he was missing a finger care of the douchebags from the Church of Liberation—but it was good enough. Next, he overlaid the cut-out wheelchair on the stairwell photo. The perspective was slightly off—the wheelchair photo was taken from a higher angle—but it was large enough to cover the clean area of the floor where it must have once sat.

Beckett stared at the collage for a second, before he finally realized what was off about the scene.

"Well, I'll be damned," he muttered.

"What? What do you see?" Dr. Nordmeyer asked, suddenly interested.

Beckett turned his nose to the sky.

"Oh, nothing. Nothing to see here. Move along."

He set the collage on the gurney and was reaching for the ME report when Dr. Nordmeyer leaned over his shoulder.

Beckett quickly slid the wheelchair cut-out beneath the stairwell photo. Then he started to whistle as he flipped through the pages of notes.

No evidence of debris from a weapon found in any of the lacerations.

"Oh, really."

Beckett reached for a speculum and proceeded to spread one of the deeper wounds on the man's scalp. With it spread wide, he used forceps to peek around. He went as far as to tap the man's exposed bone but didn't find any debris.

"Hmm."

He set about tackling another one of the cuts next, this time focusing on the largest and deepest. Just when he thought he saw something, a tiny fleck of gray, the speculum, which was slightly too small for this wound, slipped and popped out.

"Fuckin' hell," he muttered as he rammed it back in again, harder and deeper this time.

Thankfully, he spotted what looked like a small gray fiber, only three or four millimeters long. The speculum started to slip again, but he managed to grab the fiber and pull it before the wound snapped closed.

"*No evidence of debris from a weapon found in any of the lacerations*, huh?" he mocked as he held the tiny fiber up to the light. "Then what the hell is this?"

Chapter 42

HANNA SMOOTHED THE FRONT OF her dress and tried to walk as stately as possible up the long front staircase leading to the entrance of the Loomis Estate. At some point, a man—a *gentleman*—attempted to take her arm with a gloved hand, but she shook him off, fighting back a scornful remark.

She settled on, "It's twenty nineteen, dear." She thought the thick, southern accent was a good touch.

The man, who had one of those gray mustaches with the twirly ends looked at her as if she'd just taken a dump on the hood of his Bentley.

Hanna smiled and continued up the steps.

Halfway to the top, her eyes fell on the two men that were checking the guest list as people approached; on the left was a burly black man who was bald and had close-set eyes, while the other was Leroy Walker.

No, that's not right, she scorned herself. *That's not Leroy, that's C.J. Yobooty.*

Even her thoughts had a southern accent now as she fell completely into the role.

Meryl Streep would be so proud.

Hanna deliberately made her way to the right side of the staircase so that she could have her name checked off the list by Leroy. But just as she was about to grab the railing, a man and a woman—the former looked like the Great Gatsby while the latter a porn star—giggled and forced their way in front of her.

For a second, she envisioned her foot sliding out and clipping the back of the Jenna Jameson's Jimmy Choos, sending her flying to the ground.

Instead, she brought a hand to her lips and muttered, "Oh, dear," and let them pass.

"Alright, not so thick, Hanna," Screech muttered in her ear.

Hanna couldn't help but smile.

The duo went to Leroy and he dutifully checked off their names.

"Ma'am, over here please," the other security guard said, gesturing for Hanna to come on his side.

Hanna stopped smiling. She watched as Leroy's brow furrowed and he searched for the couple's names.

Hurry up, C.J.

"Ma'am?"

Shit.

Hanna couldn't stall any longer. She moved to the other side of the staircase and pulled the envelope with the invitation from her clutch.

"Name?" the man said, not even bothering to look at the invitation.

"Greta Armatridge," she said, slowly shifting her shoulders and pouting with her lips.

I should get an Oscar for this shit.

The man scanned his list then said, "Thank you, go on inside."

Hanna just stood there, invitation in hand. She couldn't believe it.

You mean after all this shit, I could've just said I was anybody on that list? Instead, I get to be an eighty-year-old grandma?

"Ma'am, would you please continue up the steps? You're holding up the line."

Hanna made a mental note to slap Screech and then hurried up the steps, making sure to glide in front of the bimbo and her sugar daddy.

The house, quite frankly, was like nothing she'd ever seen outside of the movies.

The entrance was grand, but that was only the beginning; there was a chandelier in the front hall that must have weighed a metric ton and require the services of a small powerplant to fuel all of the lights.

Hanna tried to act normal, tried to pretend like she'd seen this before—*Oh, gee all this for little ol' me? For my debutante ball?*—but everything was just so... *grand*, that it gave her pause.

"Strip club rules, remember?" Screech said in her ear.

Hanna frowned and started deeper into the house, admiring the wooden floors that were polished enough to act as mirrors and the gilded frames on paintings made by dead French people, the names of whom she did not know.

Fitting in here would prove difficult, but her one skill, the thing that she'd been gifted with ever since her mother had abandoned her at the side of the road when she was eleven, was to get other people to believe in her, to do what she wanted. It was a skill necessary for survival.

Even before her master's degree, Hanna had had significant insight into the human condition. The reality was, the vast majority of people were intractable in their beliefs and opinions. So long as you did nothing to directly contradict them, they were apt to go along with many a narrative. This was most evident while conversing; most people weren't listening, they were simply rehearsing their responses in their head as the other party spoke. Sure, they were having a conversation, but not with you.

They were conversing with themselves.

And so long as you just filled in the blanks, ticked all the right boxes, they wouldn't question anything. These were just plastic people with plastic faces and plastic lives.

Hanna often wondered what it must be like for these people when they realized that the only real thing about them is the number of zeroes in their bank account.

It saddened her that most people lost before they even knew the rules or how to play the game.

She'd taken only a few more steps into the hallway when a man approached her from the side. But unlike the man who'd attempted to help her up the stairs, this clearly wasn't hired help; the person approaching her was young and handsome, mid-thirties, maybe, dressed in a sharp white shirt, black bowtie, and black suit jacket. He had the beginnings of a beard, not in the manicured way, but a genuine five o'clock shadow.

"Hi there," he said, with a grin. Hanna noted that the smile didn't quite reach his eyes.

She knew at that moment that this man wasn't like the others, that like her, he didn't quite fit in.

Hanna just hoped that he didn't see the same in her.

"You come alone?"

"I did," she replied with a nod, falling just short of batting her eyelashes.

"Good," he replied, "so did I."

An uncomfortable silence ensued, and Hanna chewed her lip while fighting the urge to say something.

You're the debutante here, sweetheart, the voice of a fictional Southern grandmother reminded her. *Let the boys come to you. It's your flower they want, so let them sniff it before they pluck it.*

She inadvertently shuddered.

"Yeah, that's the way I feel, too," the man said before extending his hand. "Mackenzie Wilcox."

Hanna knew at once that it was a fake name. She smiled.

"Greta, Greta Armatridge."

They shook hands.

"Well, *Greta*, would you like something to drink? Because I sure as hell would."

For the first time since meeting the man, Hanna detected that he was being sincere.

"I thought you'd never ask."

Chapter 43

Diego screamed, his mouth extending beyond normal limits in sheer agony.

"Dane!" Drake yelled, pulling his cutlass from the sand.

Dane didn't even look at him. He simply grimaced, and with a heavy yank, pulled the cutlass free from Diego's calf. Blood immediately spurted forth from a gash that had nearly severed the man's foot.

Drake's first instinct was to run to Diego, but when Dane raised the cutlass high above his head for a second time, he changed his approach. Instead, he ran at his brother, intent on tackling him, on driving his shoulder into his solar plexus and ending this insanity.

But Dane didn't hack Diego's other leg; with his free hand, he reached down and grabbed a tuft of the man's greasy hair and pulled his head up.

Oblivious to Drake's approach, Dane leaned in close and growled in the man's ear.

"Where is he? Where's Smith?"

The question made Drake pause, his own grip on the worn handle of the cutlass loosening.

Diego's eyes rolled back in his head, which made Dane pull even harder. The wounded man cried out and lucidity returned to his features.

"*El phantasmo*," Diego gasped.

Dane gritted his teeth and pulled harder, hard enough that the man's Adam's apple jutted unnaturally from his throat.

"Where's Ken Smith? Where's Wesley Smith?" Dane demanded in an oddly calm voice.

Drake was still shocked by what had happened, but he realized that there was a rhyme and reason to his brother's madness.

His methodology was insane, of course, but it *was* going to get them somewhere. It *had* to.

Drake swallowed hard and stopped several feet from Diego.

"Tell him," he urged. "Tell him—tell *us*—where Ken Smith is."

Diego's wide eyes darted to the cutlass in Drake's hand.

"Please," he begged, eyes still locked on the blade.

Drake gave the cutlass a small twist, a subtle gesture, but enough for the metal to catch a beam of light.

"Tell us where they are," he ordered with more authority this time.

Diego had started to wheeze, partly because of the angle of his windpipe, but also because of the wound that continued to weep blood into the tall grass.

Drake looked to his brother and gave him a subtle nod. Dane returned the gesture and then eased his grip on the man's hair.

"Last chance," Drake said, "tell us where they are."

"The church," Diego managed to gasp. "They're at the church. The *Iglesia de Liberacion*."

Even given his limited understanding of Spanish, Drake understood.

Iglesia de Liberacion… the Church of Liberation. The place where Ken Smith had first met—and rescued—Raul. The place where this all began and where it would surely end.

How fitting, Drake thought. *After traveling more than—*

There was another glint of steel, only this time it came from Dane's blade and not his own. Drake was only three or four feet from his brother and Diego, and yet that was three or four feet too far.

He watched in horror as his brother twisted his fingers in Diego's hair and then pulled as hard as he could. The man gasped or burped or some other visceral noise emerged from his throat a split-second before Dane slid the sharp edge of the cutlass across the man's flesh.

"No!" Drake screamed, "*No!*"

But he was too late. Dane let go of Diego's head and it smashed to the ground, blood spurting from the crimson smile.

Chapter 44

BECKETT PULLED HIS HEAD BACK from the computer monitor.

"What the hell?"

He did a side-by-side comparison of the image he'd found on the Internet and that of the item that he'd pulled from Mr. Armatridge's head wound.

It was an exact match. It wasn't just a *close* match, identical. Beckett was by no means a fiber analyst, but he knew a perfect match when he saw one.

Feeling his headache returning, Beckett pinched the bridge of his nose and turned around to look at Dr. Nordmeyer.

Only she wasn't there.

"Where'd you go?" he asked the empty office.

The doctor had made it clear that she wasn't happy about him re-evaluating one of her cases, with good reason. But that didn't bother Beckett. What gave him pause was the subtle threat that she might do the same with his.

And one case in particular—the Winston Trent suicide—might be off just enough for others to start asking questions that might prove difficult to answer.

But he couldn't exactly stop what he was doing, not now, not after what he already found.

Sure, the request had come from Screech, but it was all him now. He liked Screech, liked him quite a lot, actually. And the man knew things about him, things that no one else knew. The man had already proven that he could be trusted after what had happened in the Virgin Gorda, but when times got tough… people's mouths started to run.

No, that's not right. When times get tough, the tougher get times.

He shook his head and then immediately regretted it. It only served to exacerbate his throbbing skull.

"Shit," he grumbled, realizing that he must have drifted off for a moment or two.

He blinked and reconfirmed what he'd seen on the screen. Then he pulled up a series of photographs from the inside of Mrs. Armatridge's house. Normally, he would have had to put in a formal request with the NYPD or DA for images not directly related to the body or scene of the crime, but Screech had somehow gotten his hands on them and sent them his way.

He scrolled through the photos until he found one that showed the back of the house, the area from which Mrs. Armatridge claimed to have entered prior to finding her husband.

As expected, there wasn't just a single door, but a whole bay of glass doors, at least fifteen feet wide, that were folded up like a compressed accordion.

This is crazy, he thought. *You're being crazy, Beckett.*

But the evidence was irrefutable.

The opening in the back of Mrs. Armatridge's house was large enough for many a creature to find their way in. A cat, a stray dog, even a raccoon.

Beckett went back to the image of the item he found in the wound and exhaled sharply.

Or an owl... an owl could definitely have come through those doors.

Chapter 45

"HUH," MACKENZIE SAID AS HE handed Hanna her drink. "For some reason, I pictured you as more of a scotch on the rocks-type girl."

Hanna looked down at the colorful cocktail in her hand and tried to keep a straight face.

"Oh, no," she said in a Southern accent, "Sex on the Beach."

The man raised an eyebrow, but then let her be and sipped his old-fashioned.

As they drank, Hanna turned her back to the bartender and surveyed the room. It was filling up now, with more people arriving every minute. They all looked the same to her; all fake smiles and real jewelry. As she surveyed the crowd, Hanna made sure to direct the center of her chest, which was adorned with Screech's tacky camera pendant, at their faces. It was a little awkward, but she figured that this display might be overlooked as some sort of debutante presenting ritual.

So far, she saw nobody out of the ordinary, nobody of interest.

Definitely no Steffani Loomis.

"Well, shall we?" Mackenzie asked.

Hanna looked at him, awaiting clarification. With a smile on his handsome face, he waved a hand toward the hallway that most people were generally moving towards.

"The auction."

When Hanna still didn't know what he was talking about, Mackenzie added, "The silent auction for charity?"

Hanna smiled warmly.

"Oh, but of course."

When he held out his arm, she took it and allowed herself to be led away from the bar. She left the horrible saccharine drink behind.

"Hanna, come on, you sound like Honey Boo Boo for Christ's sake. Just be normal, look around and get the hell out of there," Screech whispered in her ear.

To Hanna, he seemed nervous, but looking around, she couldn't see why. These people were harmless, little plastic Barbies and Kens.

Besides, she liked this Mackenzie character. Sure, he was lying to her, to everyone, but there was something interesting about him. Something unique in this setting.

"So, what do you do, Mackenzie?" she asked warmly as they maneuvered around several slow walkers. While she was waiting for him to answer, she continued to take in the crowd, trying to locate Steffani. The problem was, Hanna didn't know what the woman looked like. Steffani had stopped posting on social media years ago, and while Screech had managed to recover some archived images, Hanna suspected that the woman looked very different now than from her wilder, college years. Especially given this hoity-toity environment.

"I fix things," Mackenzie said at last.

Interesting.

This wasn't the reply she was expecting; there was too much honesty in it.

"So, you're a handyman."

Mackenzie smirked.

"Something like that; I am good with my hands, after all."

Hanna feigned embarrassment by batting her eyelashes. She stopped just shy of puffing her hair.

Mackenzie led her into a room that was something of a great hall, complete with a chandelier that matched the one in the front entrance. The walls were covered in paintings, all of which were bathed in soft lights. The sheer number of works was dazzling, and Hanna slowed.

It was like stepping into a private museum, not a charity auction.

"You're an art lover?" Mackenzie asked, picking up on her change in pace.

"I like to dabble."

They started on the left, planning on making their way around the room clockwise. This would allow them to pass the greatest number of people and also permit Hanna to look at the paintings. While she wasn't an 'art lover' *per se*, she actually did enjoy certain pieces. Mackenzie led her to the first painting, beneath which there was a small table with a security guard seated beside it.

This particular painting wasn't to Hanna's liking; it was far too realistic, depicting a scene from somewhere in the Hamptons, she presumed. She glanced at it briefly, then let her eyes drift down to the auction sheet beneath.

For the second time in just over a minute, her jaw dropped.

The leading bid, despite the fact that guests had just started to arrive, had already reached the low six figures.

"Not my taste," Hanna said quickly, trying not to make her sticker shock obvious. "Come on, show me something more… abstract."

"Sure," Mackenzie replied, taking a sip of his scotch.

Arm in arm, they walked past a series of photorealistic paintings until they came upon one that caught Hanna's eye.

It was a fairly basic whitewashed oil painting, in the center of which was a red dot. There were several other smaller dots arranged in a semi-circle around the central one. It was a simple painting, but there was an elegance to it and a detail to each of the dots that made them unique. Hanna could see the individual brushstrokes, and it took all her effort not to reach out and touch them. She wasn't sure what it was about this painting, but it had a way of drawing her in. Maybe it was the brushstrokes or something else entirely; whatever it was, Hanna could visualize the artist hunched over, meticulously crafting those small circles.

"I like this one," Mackenzie said in an uplifting tone.

"Me too," Hanna admitted, her eyes still locked on the painting.

As soon as her eyes started to drift downward, her earpiece crackled to life.

"Don't even think about it, Hanna," Screech warned.

Hanna ignored him, wishing that she'd opted for the model with a mute switch.

The artist was someone by the name of Hiro Maki Suduki, whom she'd never heard of. And, judging by the paucity of bids, she assumed that not many others had, either. Hanna looked around the room for a moment, observing the other two dozen or so couples paying attention to the photorealistic oil paintings of scenery and fruit and other inane objects.

But this one…

She looked at the center dot again, concentrating on the brushstrokes, imagining now that it wasn't the artist making them, but her.

Without thinking, she reached for the pen beside the sheet of paper.

"Hanna. *Hanna.* Don't do it. Don't."

A smirk formed on her face.

You made me wear this stupid dress, come to this pretentious ball, wear makeup for Christ's sake, and now it's payback time.

Still grinning, she wrote a number that was much larger than the previous bid.

"Whoa," Mackenzie exclaimed as he peered over her shoulder. "You *really* like this painting."

Hanna looked at him.

"Yeah, I guess I do. There's something—" movement out of the corner of her eye caught her attention and she stopped speaking.

The smile vanished.

It was Steffani Loomis, there was no question about it. The woman was tall and lean and breathtakingly beautiful. While she wasn't much older than Hanna herself, she walked with an air of someone who'd lived a lifetime already.

The word that Drake had used so many times in describing Ken Smith and those involved in ANGUIS Holdings came to mind.

As the woman ran a hand through her blond hair and took a sip of her Martini, Hanna couldn't help but think that that word was the perfect one to describe Steffani Loomis.

This woman had *power*.

And for a moment, for a fraction of a second, the sight of her was so intoxicating that Hanna *wanted* that power for herself.

"Greta? You okay?"

Hanna nodded and casually unhooked her arm from Mackenzie's.

"Yeah, I'll be fine. I just saw someone I recognized. Wait here for me, would you?"

Before Mackenzie could answer, Hanna hurried after Steffani Loomis, while Screech protested relentlessly in her ear.

Chapter 46

DRAKE'S ENTIRE BODY WENT COLD. He couldn't believe what he'd just seen, what his brother had done.

Dane had killed a man in cold blood. Diego had already given up the information they needed, and yet Dane hadn't hesitated in slitting his throat. Sure, Diego was the one who had given Drake up to Wesley Smith, but he didn't deserve to die. He was just a man trying to survive, trying to make sure his family wasn't targeted.

And Dane had killed him.

"Let's go, I know where the church is," Dane said, as he wiped the cutlass blade off on Diego's pants. Blood was still gurgling from the wound in his neck, albeit slower than it had a few seconds ago.

Drake blinked. He was unable to move, unable to speak.

His brother took three steps toward the jungle before realizing that Drake wasn't following him. He turned and glared at him.

"He was suffering," Dane said simply. When Drake still didn't so much as fidget, he added, "What did you want me to do? Just leave him here? Let him bleed out slowly, die a horrible death? Suffer even more?"

Drake's jaw fell open, but he still couldn't speak.

Dane's eyes dropped to Diego's head, and he focused on the stained grass, the chuff of blood as the man's heart completed its final, labored contractions.

"I didn't want him to suffer," he said in a strange voice. It wasn't remorse, not quite, but sadness. A deep, brooding sadness. "I don't want anybody to suffer."

At long last, Drake got his voice back.

"Suffer? *Suffer?*" he nearly shouted. "You're the one who hacked his leg... *you're* the one who made him suffer. You didn't have to do that, you didn't have to kill him. He told us what we wanted!"

The expression on his brother's face didn't change.

"I didn't make him suffer," he said flatly.

Drake ground his teeth and tightened his grip on his cutlass before raising it high above his head. He took a menacing step forward.

"You killed him!"

He expected his brother to raise his own cutlass, which was still stained with Diego's blood, or at the very least defend his actions.

The man did neither.

Dane simply stood there, his eyes darting from Drake's face to the cutlass glinting in the midmorning sun. It was almost as if he was silently daring Drake—no, not daring, *begging*—to deliver the final blow.

Drake closed his eyes and lowered the blade.

"What happened to you, Dane?" he whispered, choking back a sob. "What the hell happened to you?"

Dane strode forward and grabbed Drake by the collar and shook his eyes open.

"What happened to me? *What happened to me?* I see the world for what it is, Drake. I've seen suffering on a magnitude you couldn't even imagine. I've seen people skinned alive. I've seen people get their genitals chopped off and fed to them. I've seen women and children mowed down in the streets."

Drake tried to back away, but his brother's grip tightened, and he pulled him even closer.

"I saw a woman struggling every day to breathe, begging for death. I saw a man—no, not a man, a *boy*—murder his mother and father."

Drake swallowed hard.

"That boy, that boy was Ray, wasn't it? He was the one who—"

Dane pulled him so close now that their noses were nearly touching.

"I saw my best friend kill his own family to stop their suffering."

With that, Dane lowered his eyes and finally shoved Drake away from him.

Tears welled in Drake's eyes.

Ray had murdered his mother and father and then he'd become a zealot, someone who was determined to end suffering in any and every way he knew how. *That* was why Dane left.

Because he didn't want to be like his friend.

But now that Ray was gone, Dane had filled the void he left behind.

When you've come to the conclusion that the world is an Erebus of suffering, it was no great feat to justify your actions.

Like slitting a man's throat.

"Suffering is everywhere, Drake. And only once you come to terms with that fact, will you be liberated."

Liberated...

The word struck a chord with Drake for more reasons than one.

"Let's end this," Dane said as he started toward the jungle again. "Let's end this suffering once and for all."

Chapter 47

DR. KAREN NORDMEYER GAWKED.

"This is a joke, right?"

Beckett mimicked her walleye expression.

"An owl? Are you drunk?"

"Not at present, no. Although, to be honest, I would much rather be drunk than sitting here talking to you."

Dr. Nordmeyer blinked rapidly and ignored his comment.

"You're going to go ahead and write a new report about Mr. Armatridge's death, contravening what I wrote, what you told me to write? You're going to state that Mr. Armatridge wasn't pushed by his wife and brained on the stairs—which is what you told me initially—but that an owl flew in from outside, clawed his fucking head, and then flew off again without anybody seeing it?"

Beckett rocked his head from side to side.

"Yep. That's what I'm going to write."

Dr. Nordmeyer threw her head back in frustration.

"That's bullshit—*this* is bullshit."

"Nope, it's the truth. Look, I get it, you alpha female types don't like getting things wrong. But—"

She glared at him.

"Me? *Me?* You told me—"

"Potayto, Potato. Hakuna Matata. There's blood spatter on the back of the man's wheelchair. There is no way that blood could have gotten there if he was pushed *forward*. And I found a piece of an owl feather embedded in his scalp. Moreover, my dear Watson, the wounds are consistent with owl claw marks. And, sorry to say, but this isn't the first time that an owl has attacked somebody with the same claw pattern. What I say, is that we should put an APB out for Hedwig, ASAP, what do you think?"

Nordmeyer thought about killing him at that moment, or so Beckett surmised.

"This isn't going to look good, Dr. Campbell."

Beckett stared at her.

"Look at me," he instructed, indicating his dyed hair and the tattoos running up his arms. "Does it look like I give a shit what anything *looks* like? No, and you shouldn't either. What you should give a shit about, is making sure you do your job properly."

"But you told me, you said—"

"And Michael Jackson's doctor told him to take those pills. He still ended up dead, didn't he?"

"What?"

Beckett was starting to get frustrated now. He had more important things to expend his mental energy on, like planning a trip with Suzan.

Or adding a new tattoo to his collection, perhaps.

"I don't give a fuck who told you what happened. Me, the Pope, Steven Tyler; I don't care. It's what *actually* happened that matters. And Armand Armadillo or whatever the hell his name is was killed by an owl, not his wife. It was an accident. You want to report me to the review board? If you really think I'm wrong here, *do it*. I give zero fucks about that. I mean, I already know those assholes by name, anyway. So, go on, do it. Or you can put on your big boy pants, go out and drown your sorrows with a Crantini, do some goat yoga, whatever, *and get over it*."

Dr. Nordmeyer's mouth fell open.

"This is the report that I'm submitting," he said with what he hoped sounded like finality. To emphasize his point,

Beckett spun around and started from the room, intent on making a copy to give to Screech before he submitted it to Sgt. Yasiv and his team.

And then he would tell Screech that this was it, that this was the last time he was going to do the kid any favors.

In his mind, Beckett was already planning this conversation, thinking that no matter what Dr. Nordmeyer said, he would ignore her.

But then she said the one thing that could give him pause.

"That's how it's going to be, then? How would you like it if someone started digging into your old cases, Beckett? Digging up all your dirty laundry?"

His footsteps faltered, but only briefly.

"Yeah," he said in a much softer tone as he pulled the door wide and stepped into the hallway. "You do that. You see where that gets you."

Chapter 48

HANNA HURRIED AFTER STEFFANI LOOMIS, tucking her chin to her chest as she moved.

"Screech? You ready for this?" she whispered.

"What? Ready for what? Just observe, Hanna."

Yeah, right.

Hanna picked up the pace. Steffani was now just a dozen strides from her, and she was closing the distance fast.

"There's no way that I got dressed up and then not have any fun."

She heard a grunt.

"Leroy, look after her."

Hanna rolled her eyes.

Amateurs.

"Still me, douchebag."

Screech swore.

"Don't do it, Hanna. Please."

She heard a click, and then radio silence.

Well, listening to men never got me anywhere, so why would I start now?

"Steffani," she called. The woman in front of her slowed but didn't turn. "Steffani!"

This time, the woman stopped and spun on her heels. She was indeed attractive, with a strong jaw, straight nose, and eyes that seemed to sparkle even in the dim hallway.

"Yes?" she said. "Can I help you?"

"You don't… you don't remember me, do you?" Hanna said, feigning being hurt.

Steffani shook her head.

"I'm afraid not. I meet a lot of people in my line of work, and I was never good at names." Yet despite her words,

Steffani took a step forward and Hanna noticed that the woman's right arm twitched, as if she was preparing to shake hands.

Most people would have seen this as nothing more than an involuntary movement, but Hanna wasn't like most people. She saw it as an invitation.

"Well, I'm not really from this line of work," Hanna said casually, raising her hands and gesturing to the ornate hallway in which they stood. "We went to high school together."

Screech, you better be listening…

Steffani's brow furrowed and she inspected Hanna more closely.

"Greta Armatridge… We were at—" The mic in her ear clicked on suddenly, giving Hanna the answer that she needed. —"Pinedale Heights. Don't you remember?"

Another micro expression, this one confirming that Steffani had indeed attended Pinedale Heights. Hanna decided to grab onto this thread and pull, even if it meant unraveling the entire sweater.

"We were in science class together—Mrs. Trottier's class." This was pure bullshit, but Hanna knew that if she showed confidence, then the other party was likely to accept her claim. "No, no that's not right. *I* was in Mrs. Trottier's class, you were in the other science class."

Steffani nodded, but to Hanna's surprise, she held back from completely accepting this narrative.

She's careful, guarded. I would be too if I was in charge of a heroin smuggling ring.

"What did you say your name was again?"

Hanna made sure her smile never slipped.

"Greta Armatridge," she replied.

"Huh. Well, it was nice to see you again," Steffani said, hooking a thumb over her shoulder as she spoke. "But I need to get moving, I've got something to do for the auction. Please, make yourself at home. If you need anything, be sure to ask the waitstaff. They'll get you anything you need."

With a curt nod, Steffani receded down the hallway.

Hanna watched her go. When she was out of sight, the smile slid off her face.

"You get all that, Screech?" she whispered. "Cool as a cucumber, that one."

"Get the fuck out of there, Hanna. Get out of there before someone makes you. This was supposed to be an observational mission, you weren't supposed to interact with the mark."

Hanna once again rolled her eyes, this time at the use of the terms mission and mark.

Both Screech and Leroy were making this out to be more exciting than it really was. It was as if they were trying to turn it into a *Mission Impossible* movie. Now only if Mackenzie was about six inches shorter and had a beak on him like a toucan, they'd be pretty close.

"Relax, act like you've done this before," Hanna shot back as she turned and started to follow after Steffani. "Besides," she continued, finding an open door to what looked like a study, "the woman said to make myself at home, didn't she?"

Before waiting for Screech to answer, Hanna pushed the door wide and slipped inside.

Chapter 49

DRAKE WANTED TO RUN. HE wanted to leave his brother and this nightmare somewhere deep in the Colombian jungle and never return.

His brother had murdered a man who had turned Drake in so that he could protect his own family.

The worst part? The worst part was that Dane had done all of this without even skipping a beat.

But Drake had logistical and psychological barriers. He didn't know how to get out the jungle, and he knew that if he left without confronting Ken Smith, the nightmare would never end.

In the end, he fell into line behind his brother, half-heartedly chopping at the vegetation to clear their path. They walked for hours, the sun reaching its apex before languidly beginning its descent. To Drake, it felt as if they were walking in a giant circle or not even moving at all; everything just looked the same. At one point, he even came across strange markings on a crooked sapling that he could've sworn he made himself with his cutlass hours ago.

They moved mostly in silence. Every once in a while, Dane grunted and pointed at something in the distance or a particularly nasty thorned bush to avoid, but Drake barely heard him.

It dawned on him that he was at the complete and utter mercy of his brother.

And this feeling of helplessness was frightening.

With this in mind, Drake wiped sweat from his eyes and looked up. His brother had paused about five paces ahead of him, raising his cutlass high in the air. As he did, Drake saw blood on the blade, even though that was impossible given that they'd been hacking through the jungle for hours now. And yet he saw it, he saw it as clearly as he saw Diego's Adam's apple jutting out of his throat seconds before it was sliced by this very blade.

A shudder ran through him, and he tried to distract himself by sipping on his canteen of water.

He finished the last drop.

"I'm dry," he croaked.

Dane turned around, glanced at his canteen and then slipped his own from his shoulder. He tossed it to Drake.

"One more day," he said.

Drake stopped mid-sip.

"Another day?"

Dane looked at him with a neutral expression and then nodded.

"We need to set up camp before dark. We won't be able to sleep in the open like last night; too deep in the jungle now."

Drake felt a headache coming on, which in turn reminded him of the pain in his side, of his damaged liver.

"What the fuck, Dane. What's out here? Jungle cats? Bears?"

When the same dull expression remained in the man's eyes, Drake began to question whether or not this was indeed his brother. How can this be the same person who came with Screech to save me from Ray Reynolds? How can this be the same person that I used to ride bikes with, play cards, run through the sprinkler?

The man was empty.

But are we really that different? Drake wondered suddenly. He wasn't empty, that was certain; he was full of rage and resentment toward Ken Smith.

All the other things in his life, however, had been pushed to the wayside. Ignored, abused, neglected. Shit, he had a son that he hadn't seen but for five minutes. He'd also nearly sent a young boy to his death just so that he could infiltrate a gang of street thugs. He'd coerced a woman into helping him break out of a psychiatric facility, letting a known serial killer loose in the process. He'd failed Chase when she was struggling with her addiction and needed him most.

And then there was Clay.

Clay, his best friend, the person who, for many years, meant the most to him in the entire world. He'd let him down, too. Got him killed by not protecting his back.

For what?

For the Skeleton King? A fable? A crutch upon which to place all his problems?

Are we really all that different, Dane? When it boils down to it?

Sure, Drake wasn't empty. But what would happen after his showdown with Ken Smith, should it take place here on this foreign soil, in this jungle?

"No, I'm not scared of the animals," Dane said, turning his eyes forward once more.

Drake didn't need to ask what frightened his brother, and not just because he knew Dane would eventually finish his sentence.

No, he already knew what his brother was afraid of because it was what he feared most as well.

"I'm afraid of people," Dane said, his tone softening for the first time in hours. "I'm afraid of what people can do."

So am I, Drake thought. *So am I.*

Chapter 50

BECKETT SQUINTED UP AT THE address that Screech had given him over the phone.

What the hell?

Not only were they no longer working out of a condemned building, but it wasn't even Triple D Investigations anymore. No, it was some acronym—DSLH—that he'd never seen before. Folder in hand, he had to knock on the door three times before a tired-looking Screech opened it. He had some sort of Bluetooth device jammed in his ear and he was practically scowling.

"Beckett," he said with a nod.

Beckett said hello and then waited for Screech to step aside and allow him to enter. The man surprised him by doing neither.

Okay, it's going to be like that, then.

He glanced over Screech's shoulder, trying to get a glimpse of Drake in the background, but so far as he could see, the new digs, as impressive as they were, were empty.

Just as well, he thought. Things had been strained between him and Drake, and with what was going on in his personal life, Beckett wasn't sure that having Drake as an acquaintance let alone friend was in either of their best interests.

Beckett held the folder out to Screech, but someone must've said something in his ear, because he suddenly looked off to one side, the corners of his lips pulling down even further.

"Observe only," he hissed, grabbing the folder. He tried to pull it away, but Beckett held fast.

"This is the last favor I'm doing for you, Screech," Beckett said, offering his own severe and unwavering expression.

Screech nodded and yet Beckett still didn't relinquish his grip on the folder.

"One more thing," he continued.

"Yeah? What?" Screech asked. Something crossed his eyes, not just distrust and unease, but something more primal.

Fear.

That's good, Beckett thought. *He* should *fear me.*

He shook his head; that was just the headache talking. He wouldn't do anything to Screech, unless...

"I wasn't the only one looking into this case."

"Really? Who else was looking into it?"

Beckett shrugged. He'd seen a red flag on Dr. Nordmeyer's report, meaning that it had been accessed recently. His first thought was that it was just Sgt. Yasiv, or the DA, or even Dr. Nordmeyer herself, but when he'd investigated further, he saw that this wasn't the case.

"Some law office, Smith, Smith, and Johnson or something. Don't know if it means anything, I just thought I'd give you a heads-up."

He let go of the folder and Screech took it. He was so preoccupied that Beckett wasn't sure the man had heard him. Without even a thank you, Screech closed the door.

"You're welcome," Beckett grumbled as he made his way back to the car.

As he took up residence behind the wheel, a sudden sadness and loneliness overcame him. He'd been friends with Drake for nearly a decade and, at times like these, he missed the man. He missed Drake's serious demeanor, but he also missed sharing drinks with him and shooting the shit.

He liked doing that with Dr. Ron Stransky as well, but he'd ended that friendship, too. And there was no going back on that one.

He wondered briefly if there would be a time when he and Drake could reconnect, share a beer once again as they'd done in the old days.

Something in the back of Beckett's mind, something mixing with his headache, told him that that was unlikely. The path that his life had taken him on after a chance meeting with Craig Sloan was a divergent path; a lonely, desperate path.

Beckett's fingers started to tingle, making it difficult to pull out his cell phone and dial a number. He managed and after two rings, a female voice answered.

"Suzan? It's Beckett. I think we should go on that vacation now. But I'm thinking about going somewhere warm."

Somewhere warm, but also a place where I can add to my tattoos.

Chapter 51

"JUST OBSERVE," SCREECH REITERATED IN Hanna's ear.

Hanna, as she'd done with the last dozen requests, ignored him. This was her gig, she set the rules.

She found herself in an office complete with a large desk in the middle of the room. There was no computer on the desk, but there was a folder. However, any thoughts of a slam dunk—photos of Steffani standing on a street corner, heroin brick in hand, perhaps—were dashed when she saw that it was only images of a building adorned with the name *Hart Investigator*. Still, she made sure that all of this was picked up by the camera around her neck.

Hanna tried the drawers next, but they were all locked. She debated trying to pick them, but with the noise picking up outside the room, she decided not to press her luck. Instead, she turned around and stepped toward the bookshelf.

Encyclopedias? You gotta be kidding me...

She grabbed the A-D volume and pulled it out partway. When nothing happened, she shoved it back in and then moved on to the next.

"What the hell are you doing, Hanna?"

"Ever seen any spy movies? Read Nancy Drew or the Hardy boys? I'm looking for a secret passage, that's what I'm doing," she mumbled under her breath.

"Just get out of there, go back to the auction."

Screech sounded tired now, tired and annoyed.

But his plan was flawed. Drake was somewhere halfway across the world trying to track down Ken Smith; he didn't have time for them to write down a list of names and take photos of rich people's faces. No, they needed something tangible and they needed it now. They needed something that would get Drake off the hook for *everything* that he'd done, allowing him to come back and live a normal life.

None of the books led to any secret passage, of course, and by the time Hanna got to the second row, she grew tired and bored of the charade.

"Nothing here," she grumbled.

Hanna straightened when she heard footsteps right outside the door.

Screech must've noticed the sudden change in posture from the video feed because he immediately asked her what was happening.

The footsteps were so close now that Hanna couldn't risk answering. Instead, she crouched low and scampered along the far side of the desk, and then made her way behind the partly open door. Before she could peer out, someone started to push it open, and Hanna sucked in a sharp breath and flattened her body against the wall.

"I'll be back in a minute," she heard a female voice say to someone in the hallway. "Just a minute."

And then a woman in a dress stepped into the room. Barely breathing now, Hanna watched as the woman smoothed her outfit, which, while similar to Steffani Loomis's, wasn't identical, and then started toward the desk.

Hanna followed with her eyes and then ground her teeth in frustration. She'd forgotten to put the photographs back in the folder.

"What the hell?" the woman whispered, her back still to the door.

Hanna didn't hesitate; she reached up and pulled a long metal chopstick from her hair and strode forward.

"Don't move," she said as she pressed the point to the back of the woman's neck. "Don't move and don't make a sound."

Chapter 52

DRAKE DIDN'T DARE CLOSE HIS eyes that night, even though he was beyond exhausted and his makeshift lean-to was actually quite comfortable.

His brother, on the other hand, didn't seem to have any trouble falling asleep. Within minutes of finishing laying down a bed of ferns, the man jammed his cutlass into the earth, curled up on his side, and began snoring softly.

Drake watched his brother sleep. He watched his chest slowly rise and fall, watched the man's flaccid features twitch every so often.

Clearly, taking Diego's life had done nothing to hinder his slumber.

Even though Drake had been careful not to close his eyes, he must've drifted off at some point, because the next thing he realized was that he was no longer beneath his lean-to. In fact, he wasn't even sitting.

Drake found himself hovering over his brother's body. And his hand... his right hand had started to ache.

With abstract curiosity, he looked down and noticed that he was gripping the handle of his cutlass. Not only that, but it was half-cocked, the curved blade aimed at Dane's mid-section.

Drake gasped and almost stumbled backwards. He didn't remember doing any of this.

After a deep breath, he looked down at Dane and then almost tripped again; Dane was awake and staring up at him. He didn't say anything, didn't even move. He just stared.

With considerable effort, Drake unfurled his fingers and the cutlass fell to the grass. As he retreated to his makeshift bed, he watched Dane close his eyes and slowly turn onto his other side.

There's something wrong with him, Drake thought. But as he looked up at the bright moon, he realized the same could be said about him.

That the same could be said about all of them.

Chapter 53

SCREECH SLAMMED THE DOOR CLOSED without even saying goodbye to Beckett. The man had been acting strange—stranger—than he normally was, but Screech didn't have time for that now.

He had Hanna to worry about.

"I should have never let her go," he cursed himself as he moved to his computer and stared at the video from her pendant.

Something had spooked Hanna, and she was moving quickly now, causing the video feed to stutter.

Get out of there, he pleaded silently. *Get the fuck out of there!*

But Hanna didn't appear to be going anywhere.

Screech threw the folder that Beckett had given to them on the desk without looking at it. The feeling of helplessness that came over him then was similar to how he'd felt while watching Leroy deal with the thugs in the trap house. Sure, the environment couldn't have been any more different, but in many ways, it was the same.

"Fuck," he swore.

The door opened, and the image started to rise and fall now that Hanna's breathing had become more rapid. A woman stepped through the door and started towards the desk. And then Hanna was on the move again, only she had something in her hand now. Something long and sharp and glinting.

"Don't move," Hanna said. "Don't move and don't make a sound."

Chapter 54

THE WOMAN TENSED, BUT SHE didn't lose control and start shaking or sobbing as Hanna expected she might have.

This wasn't Steffani Loomis, but it wasn't a run-of-the-mill auction participant, either.

Hanna's trade lay mostly in her ability to ply information from men, but she wasn't opposed to extracting what she wanted from a woman. And the way this woman resisted the urge to panic with a sharp object pressed to her neck by a stranger, suggested that she might be able to help them.

Hanna wasn't sure how, but she was about to find out.

In one smooth motion, she spun the woman around while keeping the needle point aimed at her throat.

She had long, straight dark hair that covered most of her face.

"Who are you?" Hanna hissed, wary of raising her voice too high in case there were others just outside the door.

The woman slowly raised a hand and brushed the hair away from her face.

Hanna gasped.

"Jasmine?"

The woman's green eyes went wide; she was clearly surprised that her assailant recognized her.

"Who are you?" Jasmine shot back.

Hanna's heart was pounding in her chest now, and she felt confusion wash over her.

"What—Jasmine, what are you doing here?" she stammered, ignoring the woman's question.

Jasmine's expression didn't falter.

"How do you know my name?"

Hanna's mouth was suddenly incredibly dry, making it difficult to swallow, let alone speak.

Jasmine, the mother of Drake's child, was here? With these people? Jasmine, ex-wife to Clay Cuthbert who had been slain by the Church of Liberation on orders of ANGUIS Holdings, had now joined them?

It didn't make sense.

"Why?" Hanna finally breathed.

Jasmine's eyes narrowed further and then they sprung open.

"Oh my god, you're with him," she said softly. "You helped Drake escape."

Confusion transitioned into anger.

"How could you? How could you betray him like this?" Hanna demanded, her voice raising an octave. "How could you do this to Drake?"

Jasmine started to shake her head.

"No, no, you don't understand. I *love* Drake. It's not what you think. I'm on *your* side."

Her response took Hanna by surprise, and she lowered the metal chopstick a little. When Jasmine took a step back, however, Hanna raised it again and ground her teeth.

"You're on *my* side? You're working with them, aren't you? You're working with Steffani Loomis and Ken Smith and all these other assholes," Hanna accused.

Jasmine was shaking her head more violently now.

"No, no, it's not like that. I'm trying to bring them down. Ever since Clay was murdered... I-I-I've been trying to infiltrate them. To figure out what they're all about and shut them down from the inside."

Hanna's upper lip curled. She didn't know what to make of this. It was a catch-22; if it was true, that would make it necessary for Jasmine to be a good liar. And if she were a good liar, there was no way to determine if she was telling the truth.

"Fuck," Hanna swore. She tilted her head to one side. "Screech, you getting this?"

She was distracted for a split-second, but that was still too long. Jasmine suddenly strode forward, and with a lightning-fast hand, she snatched the metal chopstick from Hanna.

"I'm sorry, but I'm too close."

As Hanna reached for the weapon, the door behind her flung open and thick hands grabbed her around the waist and held her tight.

As she was dragged away, Hanna heard Jasmine say, "This is an impostor… she was snooping around in here. I caught her looking through Steffani's things."

Chapter 55

LEROY WAS BORED OUT OF his mind. He'd spent the better part of the last hour checking people into the auction. People who looked exactly like one another.

Ah, the irony, he thought as he glanced down at C.J. Yobooty's ID card.

At one point, he'd stopped even bothering to look for the names that the guests gave. He simply ushered them in. What did it matter, anyway?

It's not like this was *his* job.

His partner, a much bigger and thicker man who went by the name of Trevor Bernard appeared equally as uninterested in the task.

Anything for a payday, I guess.

As the crowd slowly started to thin, Leroy turned to the other and offered something in the way of conversation. Anything to alleviate his extreme boredom.

"How long you been doing this gig for?" he asked.

Trevor grunted and looked at his watch.

"Around seven."

Great. Real conversationalist, this one.

Leroy blew air out of his mouth and stared up at the moon. He was about to ask Trevor what time they could leave this place when his earpiece crackled.

"Leroy, we've got a problem."

Leroy suddenly grew serious.

"Aha," he said, trying to make it seem like he was just confirming Trevor's answer. It only partly worked; the man was staring at him curiously.

"Something's happened... something's happened to Hanna. I need you to go check on her. Goddamn it, I said just observe."

Leroy swallowed hard and glanced over at Trevor. The man wasn't looking at him anymore; he was now talking in hushed tones into his walkie-talkie.

"Yeah, that might be difficult," Leroy said. Trevor turned back to him.

"Hey, kid, what did you say your name was again?"

Leroy glanced down at his name tag.

"C.J. Yobooty."

The man's walkie squawked, but Leroy couldn't hear the subsequent words on account of the mic in his ear acting up.

"And how old are you?"

Trevor took a menacing step forward and Leroy took an equally large step backward. Another step and his ass butted up against the wrought iron railing.

"Old enough, what is this, anyway? You want my social security? You my boss now?"

The man shook his head and continued forward. Leroy had nowhere to go now.

"Naw, but the boss, the *real* boss, he wants to see you."

"Yeah?" Leroy inquired, sliding down to a lower step. His heart was racing, and he could feel his muscles tense as he prepared to bolt. "And who might that be?"

"Major Loomis."

And that was when Leroy knew that this was a one-way street that he had to veer off. He hated the idea of leaving Hanna here by herself, but he couldn't do any good if this brute got a hold of him.

"Yeah, sure," Leroy said, trying to act casual. "No problem. Does he want to see my name tag?"

As he said this, Leroy reached down and unhooked the name tag from his shirt.

"What? Your name tag?" Trevor said with a snarl. "Why would he—"

Leroy flung the name tag like a Frisbee and it hit Trevor squarely in the face. The man cried out and Leroy used the distraction to bound down the stairs. Before his partner had even collected himself, Leroy was sprinting across the lawn, putting as much distance between him and the Loomis Estate as he could.

Chapter 56

HANNA DIDN'T STRUGGLE; THERE WAS no point. The two men who grabbed her were far stronger than she and struggling would only result in her getting a broken arm. But that didn't mean she wasn't frightened. She *was* frightened; Hanna was terrified.

She was also confused. She had no idea if Jasmine was telling the truth or if she had just been trying to save her own skin. Hanna knew full well how manipulative people could be; after all, she'd used this fact to her advantage to survive over the years. It was improbable, but not impossible, that Jasmine hooking up with Drake and even having a child with him was all part of Ken Smith's master plan.

After all, Ken had been using Drake as a pawn in his quest for power for a year or more. What better safeguard against him acting out than to control his child?

"Hanna? Hanna?"

She'd forgotten that Screech was still in her ear.

"This is my debutante ball," she almost moaned, trying to alert Screech of where she was being taken without letting the men dragging her know that she was mic'ed up. "I don't want to be taken down into a basement. I don't belong in some sort of dungeon."

One of the men held the door open while the other tried to lower her into a concrete cellar.

An all-encompassing panic struck her then.

She'd been in a basement like this before, years ago. A man had grabbed her off the street when she was only thirteen and thrown her in a cell for nearly a week before she'd managed to escape. That had been one of many close calls after her mother had abandoned her.

"Let go of me, you fucking goons," she shouted, losing her accent entirely. She kicked and thrashed, but the man switched his grip and put her in a half-nelson.

I shoulda brought a fuckin' gun. I would shoot this motherfucker in the face. I would—

"Let go of me!"

But the man didn't let go. His partner grabbed her legs and together they carried her down a rickety set of wooden stairs. This place was so different from the rest of the house that Hanna felt as if she'd been dragged into another dimension.

"What is this place?"

Her eyes darted about, and she noticed a solitary window cut out of the concrete foundation. The moon was weak, but she thought she could make out a treeline in the distance.

"Fucking trees! Is that a forest? I can see a fucking forest!"

Hanna was spun around and, before she knew what was happening, she found herself plopped down in a chair. Once again, she tried to wriggle free, but these were professionals. They used heavy leather straps to affix her legs and arms to the chair.

"Get the fuck off me!" she screamed, gnashing her teeth at any piece of flesh that came near her.

"Search her," one of the men said. The other man nodded and stepped forward.

"Get off me! Help! *Help!*"

Hanna tried to topple the chair, but it was bolted to the floor. That was when she saw the dark stains on the concrete.

Stains that could only be one thing: blood.

Her panic reached a crescendo and Hanna let out a bloodcurdling scream. Someone upstairs had to hear this, didn't they?

Rough hands were on her then, searching her from her ankles up to her thighs, unceremoniously patting down every inch of her body. When they got to her head, Hanna kept trying to hide her ear, but the man grabbed her chin with an unrelenting grip. He found the earpiece and yanked it free.

"Audio," he said simply, handing the device over to his partner.

"No!" Hanna screamed.

The man didn't even appear to take notice; he just dropped the earpiece to the ground and crushed it beneath his heel.

"She's clean," the man who'd searched her said. Without exchanging any other words, the two men started back up the stairs.

The idea of being alone down here was truly terrifying. The week that she'd been trapped in a cage, not knowing if she'd get food or water or see another face again, had been the worst of her life.

"You can't leave me here!" she thrashed so violently she became dizzy. *"You can't leave me here!"*

When the men shut off the light and left the basement, Hanna's pleas degenerated into screams.

Chapter 57

DELIRIUM HAD BEGUN TO SET IN. Drake hadn't slept at all during the night; he was too afraid of what he might do.

When the sun finally rose, and Dane awoke, he didn't mention what happened the night prior. He just set about packing up his things as if nothing had happened.

"Just a few more hours," his brother said as he looked upward as if the sky itself would lead them.

Drake nodded and prepared himself for another long slog through the jungle. He was exhausted, both mentally and physically, but something inside of him had stirred.

Excitement was an odd feeling; part anxiety, part fear, part anticipation. For Drake, his excitement was rooted in the knowledge that everything was coming to an end soon, one way or another. If his brother's estimation was correct, in a few hours, they'd be at the original Church of Liberation.

He wasn't sure if Ken or Wesley Smith would be there, if Diego had told them the truth in the moments before he'd been murdered. If they were there, there was no guarantee that he'd come out alive, or if the man who'd bested him so many times over the last few years would continue to come out on top. Drake didn't know if he would see Screech, or Jasmine, or Beckett, or even his son Clay ever again.

But he was still excited.

Excited at the prospect of ending all of this, one way or another. *That* was what held appeal to Drake.

It was just the uncertainty that made him uneasy.

Chapter 58

SCREECH LAUNCHED HIS COMPUTER MOUSE across the room in frustration. It smashed against the wall and exploded into dozens of pieces.

Jasmine was there. Jasmine, of all people, was there. *Drake's* Jasmine.

Everything became clear in the moments before the men had grabbed Hanna. Drake had been acting so strangely when it came to Jasmine and their newborn because he *knew*. He knew that she was involved in this somehow.

Screech had no idea how, but he was sure of it. And it must have torn him apart being trapped between two worlds.

He had to leave this place, not just to track down Ken but to get away from Jasmine.

Screech stared at the video stream on the computer, which was mostly dark now. When the men had yanked Hanna's earpiece, he'd lost sound, but he still had video.

Was she telling the truth? Could Jasmine really be working undercover this whole time?

He shook his head. None of that mattered now. The only thing that mattered was getting Hanna back in one piece. And now that Leroy's cover had been blown as well, that seemed like a tall task indeed.

"Goddamn observational mission," he spat through clenched teeth. "You were just supposed to observe!"

He picked up his keyboard and was about to launch it at the remnants of his mouse when the door burst open.

Screech's first instinct was to go for the gun, the pistol that Drake had given him long ago and that he kept taped to the underside of his desk. But when he saw a dark figure enter the office, sweat dripping off his forehead, Screech rocketed to his feet.

"Leroy!"

The man stumbled into the room one hand on his chest, the other in the air, indicating that he needed a moment to catch his breath.

"Goddamn it, Leroy, what's going on over there? They have Hanna!"

Leroy nodded vigorously, causing sweat to spray off him.

"I-I-I know…"

Things had gone wrong, so horribly wrong.

Screech reached for his phone and started to dial Yasiv's number before stopping halfway through.

Yasiv had warned him about this. The man had said that they were on their own with this one, that he couldn't, and wouldn't get involved. That his life would be in danger if he so much as dipped his toe in the water.

"Like it's not in danger already," he muttered as he started to dial a new number. It took three digits before he realized that he was dialing Drake's phone number. He hung up and then started a third string, but then stopped that one partway through, too.

Beckett had told him less than an hour ago that he wouldn't help him anymore.

Screech was near tears now. He had no one else to call, no chits or favors to cash in. He was on his own now.

"They've got Hanna," Leroy said, still huffing.

"I just said that."

Leroy walked over to him, still wheezing heavily.

"And they almost got me. Our first fucking job, I almost got killed. And they got Hanna."

"Goddamn it, I know! I know! *I know!*"

Leroy looked at him, silently begging for some insight, some plan of what to do next.

But Screech could offer nothing. He typically deferred to Drake for these types of decisions.

"We gotta go back," Leroy exclaimed. "You gotta get some guns or somethin' and we gotta go back. Call the police, *something*. Dude, we gotta get Hanna outta there."

Screech stared at Leroy. He is just a boy, out of his league. But so was Screech. One thing he knew for certain, is that they *couldn't* go in there guns ablazin'; they couldn't do that, because Steffani Loomis's father was a goddamn Captain in the Army. Or was. Either way, the man probably had more guns in his bedroom than they could grab by ransacking a Florida hardware store.

No, their approach had to be more subtle. They had to find a way in, but how?

The image on the computer monitor suddenly turned yellow. Someone had flicked on a single bulb in the basement where they were keeping Hanna. And now a large figure stood at the top of the stairs.

"Shit," Leroy grumbled. "This is fucked up, Screech. Somethin' bad gonna happen. We gotta get there, we gotta get there before—"

Screech hushed him and tried to focus on the screen.

"What are we going to do?" Leroy demanded. "We gotta—"

"Shut up!" Screech yelled. "Just shut the fuck up! I need to think!"

Leroy fell silent.

The figure on the top of the stairs slowly started its descent.

Leroy's right, Screech thought. *We gotta do something. And we gotta do something* now.

Chapter 59

HANNA DESPERATELY TRIED TO CLEAR the tears from her eyes and focus on the figure that was descending the stairs. Her first thought was that it was Steffani, but as it came near, she realized that this wasn't the case.

Not only was the figure not wearing a dress, but it was much larger than Steffani.

It was a man, and even though she'd never seen him before, when his deeply lined face came into view, she knew who it was.

"Hanna," he said as he approached.

"Captain Loomis," Hanna shot back without hesitation.

She expected the man to be surprised that she knew who he was, but his face gave away nothing.

"Hanna, the woman who helped Damien Drake escape from the psychiatric institution, the woman who claimed to have been raped by the Download Killer, the very same woman who'd spent her teenage years turning tricks in exchange for food and shelter."

"Fuck you," Hanna spat. The man had done his homework, she had to give him that. She thought that everyone who knew about her past had either fled the country or this earth.

But somehow this asshole had managed to dig up dirt on her.

That's fine, that's okay, she thought, trying to calm herself. *Because one day you'll be the one in chains, you and your daughter. And I'll be there watching. Taunting.*

"Yeah, Hanna... and now you're working for Drake, aren't you? Working for Drake and Screech and Leroy of all people. We've been watching you."

"And? You like what you see? Why don't you come a little closer and I'll show you a close-up?"

Again, she got the same unwavering and unfaltering demeanor from the man.

"The only question I have is what you're doing *here*. We know how you got in, pretending to be Greta Armatridge. And we know that Leroy worked the door. It wasn't really that difficult. But why? Why come here in the first place?"

Hanna pressed her lips together defiantly.

"It's for Steffani, isn't it? Yeah, that's it. I don't really know what you expected to find, though. Still, I got to give it to you guys, to Drake, for pushing Ken Smith out like that. There was a time when he and I were partners, you know. But he thought he was better than me, bigger, more powerful. What he forgot is that I was the one who helped him start this whole thing, help him get that first package out of Colombia in the casket of his fallen friend. All that power... it got to his head. But that's alright. He's gone now. And the second he left New York, I stepped in. Snatched up all of his existing trafficking routes."

Hanna said nothing; she did, however, move her shoulders so that her chest was lined up with Captain Loomis's face as his lips moved. The camera on her pendant might not have sound, but lip-reading technology had come a long way.

"It'll take time to get distribution back up again, but it'll happen. Ken's... *the* product is just too good and the price too low. People want it, Hanna. And when the demand is there, the supply shall follow. And the beauty of it? My name's not on anything. I mean, look at this place? This Estate... it's all mine, and yet I haven't signed a single paper."

Hanna still refused to speak.

"And when I'm gone, my daughter will take over for me. A Loomis legacy. She's a tough woman, smart. Determined. Unlike you, you dumb little cunt, with the proper upbringing, you can accomplish more than being just a little whore."

Hanna lost it. She spat, but it fell well short of the man's face. Then she pulled hard against the restraints on her wrists and ankles.

"Ha, touched a nerve, did I?"

For the first time since coming down those stairs, Captain Loomis's face broke into a grin.

"Yeah, I did, didn't I? I can't believe that after all these years you're still sour about what your mother did to you. Your father left you, so your mother whored you out to pay for her drug habit. Funny how these things come full circle, isn't it?"

"My father didn't leave me," Hanna fired back.

Loomis made a face.

"Oh? Is that right? I'm pretty sure he did."

"Fuck you. You and your piece of shit daughter."

Loomis chuckled.

"Yeah, you laugh. You're pathetic, hiding behind your own daughter. That's worse than what my dad did, leaving me. You're hiding not to stay out of the public eye, but because you're a coward. That's why your name never showed up with ANGUIS Holdings or the Church of Liberation. Because you're a *coward*."

Loomis's chuckle became a full-bellied laugh.

"Hanna, I've seen more death and carnage in one week than you've seen in your entire life. I've seen bodies of school children still smoldering on the ground. I've seen more horrors than you can even believe. You think you're going to get to me by calling me and my daughter names? Really?"

Hanna tried to calm herself. The man was right; he'd seen things, he'd *done* things. Getting angry and spitting insults won't affect him.

Do what you do best, play with his mind. He's a military man; he strives for control.

So, give it to him.

Hanna took a deep breath.

"Just let me go," she pleaded. The man's face twitched ever so slightly, letting her know that she was on the right path. "I'll do anything. Anything."

Loomis stepped forward.

"You're tied to a chair in a basement and no one knows you're here. I can do anything I want with or without your permission."

Hanna sighed, and she puffed out her chest.

"It's better if I give it to you rather than you taking it."

Loomis continued his approach and Hanna saw a familiar expression in his dark eyes. She'd seen it many times before.

Lust, the allure of conquest.

"And what is it that you're going to give me?"

"Anything you want."

The man's hands moved so fast that she barely saw them. Captain Loomis grabbed either side of the V of her dress and pulled hard. The material tore nearly to her navel, exposing her bra beneath. In the process, his finger snagged on her pendant and it fell to the ground.

The moment the cool air touched Hanna's bare skin, she sucked in a deep breath.

"Yeah, I bet you know what a man wants," Loomis said as he stared down at her breasts and skin that was puckered with goose pimples. Then he started to chuckle. "But you're used goods, Hanna. Used fucking goods. The only thing you can give me is an STD."

The man threw his head back and laughed.

"Yeah, yeah, maybe," Hanna said. "Or maybe it's because you don't need what I've got because your daughter gives it to you every night. I bet that little whore sucks you—"

The man lowered his head and his face contorted. It had been a long time since she'd seen such anger.

Loomis reared back with one of the massive hands he'd used to tear her dress.

Hanna heard a dull thud but was rendered unconscious before even realizing that this sound was his fist connecting with the side of her head.

Chapter 60

"I'M GONNA FUCKING KILL HIM, I'm gonna fucking kill him," Screech muttered under his breath. Without even knowing it, his hand had snaked beneath the desk and he was now gripping the butt of the pistol hidden beneath.

"We gotta hurry," was all Leroy could say.

"Think, goddamn it, Screech, think."

He'd already gone through his mental Rolodex of people he could ask for help and had come up empty. There was Mrs. Armatridge, but what the hell could she do? She was old and on house arrest.

But there had to be somebody, someone who can help. Someone who might—

A lightning of a thought crashed in his mind.

"You still have that list?" he asked.

Leroy wiped sweat from his brow.

"List? What list?"

"The list of people attending the party, did you keep it?"

Leroy patted his chest, eventually pulling out the guest list from the charity auction. Screech snatched it from him without a word.

He scanned the names, trying to find one that looked familiar, but this wasn't his crowd. He didn't recognize any of them.

But there was one person he *did* know who might fit in with this crowd. Someone who might have even performed a service for one or two of the "gentlemen".

Screech grabbed his phone from the desk and scrolled through his contacts. He found the person he was looking for and quickly clicked call.

"V," a female voice answered on the first ring.

"Veronica? It's Screech. Look, I'm desperate here. I need a favor."

"Hey Screech. A favor, huh? And all this time, I thought Mandy was more your type."

Screech ignored the comment.

"Please… I'm going to send you a list of names. You gotta tell me if you know of any of them… *please.*"

Chapter 61

HANNA'S LEFT EYE WAS SO swollen that it had sealed shut. Her right eye worked fine, but the basement was so dark that it didn't matter; she couldn't see anything. Her first instinct was to stand, but she couldn't do that either.

First confusion, then understanding.

"Help!" she croaked in a voice that didn't sound like her own. Any notion of remaining calm and collected was dashed when the only reply was her echo. "Help me!"

Hanna struggled for a few more moments but stopped when she felt the straps start to tear into the flesh on her wrists and ankles.

She looked down at herself, at her torn dress, at the dots of blood just below her collar bone. This set her off again.

All of sudden she was back in the cage, wandering back and forth like some sort of animal, shitting and pissing in a bucket.

"Help!"

Somewhere high above, she heard soft music playing.

"Help! If there's anybody up there, help me!"

A shadow to her right suddenly moved and Hanna whipped her head in that direction, her eyes bulging.

"No one can hear you down here," a female voice said as she stepped out of the darkness and into the silver moonlight from the basement's sole window.

Hanna's heart was racing again; she'd been certain that she was along.

But someone had been here the entire time.

"Steffani," Hanna hissed.

The woman took a wide berth around the chair until she was directly in front of Hanna.

"You and your little band of misfits have caused a lot of problems for us," Steffani said matter-of-factly. "More trouble than any of us would've believed. You know, we met and talked about Drake on several occasions."

The woman plucked a stray thread from her dress and flicked it onto the floor.

Hanna looked around, desperately trying to locate her necklace with the embedded video camera. Not seeing it anywhere, she decided to focus on the woman's words; if nothing else, she wanted to remember exactly what Steffani said.

"At first, Ken convinced us that it was best to keep Drake alive, that we could use him to clean up our dirty work. To be honest, I thought he was right. With men like Drake, all you have to do is set them on a path of vengeance and they'd do the rest. Ken thought that Drake would take out the competition. And if it worked, the added benefit was that we could then gain access to his brother, who had connections in South America. And it did work, at first, anyway. But then something happened. Drake lost it. I told Ken not to take out his partner, not to involve Clay, but he didn't listen to me. He rarely listened to any of us. After that night, Drake became unstable, became fixated on the Skeleton King. That's when I knew we had to sever ties with him."

In the back of her mind, Hanna acknowledged that the soft classical music upstairs had been replaced by scuffling feet.

Is that... is that Screech? Leroy?

"That Drake... he's resilient if nothing else. We tried to set up others as the Skeleton King—first that imbecile Peter Kellington, then Ray Reynolds. But nothing worked. So, there was only one play I had left: set up Ken Smith, make him the Skeleton King. And that, dear Hanna, worked better than I could have hoped. Drake did everything for me, including taking out the other members of the board: Boris, Horatio, Raul, and now Ken." Steffani laughed, a sound that grated Hanna's ears. "I was the one who put Detective Simmons up to taking the bone out of the evidence locker. I was even the one who told Officer Kramer where Drake would be that night by the hangar. Ken thought he was running the show, but I was the little birdie in his ear all along. You know how it is with men like him, whisper something in a seductive voice, and they'll think they came up with the idea. But the most important thing I did, the thing that tipped the scales in my favor, was to hide Dr. Kruk's storage locker. I was the one who changed the name on the manifest so that the police never found it. I knew that it was only a matter of time before Drake would bring him to it, and then discover the tape. But I had to wait. I had to wait to make sure that I had enough people to take over once Ken Smith went down."

Hanna was trying to take all this in, process it, but the noise upstairs was escalating.

"Did your daddy teach you how to whisper seductively in a man's ear?"

Steffani laughed again.

"Yeah, I see that you've met him already," she said, indicating the bruise on Hanna's face. "He has certain charms, that's for sure. But I run this show. *Me.*" Steffani Loomis stepped forward, bringing the item that she'd been twirling in her hand into the moonlight. "You, on the other hand," Steffani continued, spinning the metal chopstick over her thumb like some sort of magician's wand. "Are more subtle. As am I."

Steffani reached out and traced a line with the chopstick from Hanna's ear all the way down to beneath her chin.

Hanna turned her face away, but when the point dug into the soft skin between her collarbones, she moved her head straight again. There was pure hatred in the woman's eyes, and Hanna was tempted to believe her tale of deceit and deception.

"You and I are a lot alike, Hanna, and that's a problem. There's only room in this world for one of us."

She pressed the point of the chopstick deep enough to draw blood.

"You kill me," Hanna said through clenched teeth, "and my people will hunt you down. You think that power is a motivating influence? How about revenge? Because I guarantee—"

The woman withdrew the chopstick and then thrust it upward. It pierced through the soft skin beneath her chin and pinned the underside of her tongue.

Blood instantly filled Hanna's mouth and she tried to turn her head away, to escape the horrible pain that radiated upward. But Steffani reached out with her free hand and grabbed the back of her head and held it tight. Then she straddled Hanna and leaned so close that she could smell gin on the woman's breath.

"You're right, Hanna: more people *will* come. Do you think that you're the first person to be strapped to this chair?" She shook her head. "Not even close. And you won't be the last."

Hanna's eyes widened when she saw the woman's grip on the end of the chopstick tighten in her periphery. She knew that the end was near, but she didn't plead, didn't beg.

She just waited for the end.

But just before Steffani slid the spike up through her mouth and into her brain, there was a hard knock on the door above.

Steffani loosened her grip and turned her head around. There was another knock, and then the door handle started to jiggle.

"Fuck," she grumbled, sliding off Hanna. She pulled the chopstick free and now, without it plugging the wound, blood spilled freely from Hanna's mouth and soaked the front of her torn dress.

Steffani observed her for a moment, then cleaned the chopstick off on Hanna's dress before hurrying back up the stairs.

Chapter 62

SCREECH WASN'T REALLY SURPRISED THAT Veronica knew not one, but two of the guests that were attending the charity auction. What was surprising, however, was that Mandy also "knew" one of the guests.

Neither of them hesitated when Screech asked for their help; they were just happy to pay back the favor for what happened at the sex slave ring.

This is it, he thought, as he sat in his car and watched as Mandy and Veronica made their way across the street. Security had been increased after Leroy and Hanna had been found out, but that didn't matter.

Veronica and Mandy were experts at getting inside, especially given the clientele that they knew intimately.

They had no problem walking right through the gates with only a few short sentences, and then they hurried up the stairs and into the Estate.

Screech had insisted that he fit them with listening devices, but they'd refused. They'd claimed something about wanting to keep their industry secrets safe, but he had a sneaking suspicion that what they really wanted was to keep the identity of their Johns secret.

This made Screech anxious, but then he remembered just how tough these women were and, combined with the fact that Veronica had packed her trusty Taser, helped to alleviate some of his concerns.

Still, as he sat in his car with the gun resting on his lap, Screech felt rather helpless. It didn't help that Leroy was a bundle of nerves in the backseat. He was sweating bullets and kept twitching, which was driving Screech nuts. He didn't want Leroy here; he'd promised Kinesha that he wouldn't be in any danger. But there was no time to argue with the kid.

At least he knew well enough to stay quiet.

I should be in there, he thought. *I should be the one to go in there and rescue Hanna. I sent her in, after all.*

But he knew better; they knew who he was. As soon as Screech showed his face at the door, one of Loomis's goons would throw him in the basement and then both he and Hanna would be fucked.

No, he had to wait.

Screech took a deep breath and then pulled out his phone and stared at the screen.

Yasiv had told him that he couldn't get involved in this, but that didn't mean that *everyone* in law enforcement had to stay out of it.

After contacting Veronica, Screech had racked his brain for someone in the NYPD that he could trust. Yasiv being out meant that Detective Dunbar was also a no go, which left only Officer Kramer. He'd considered it but based on what Yasiv had said about the man's unrelenting desire to see Drake in prison, Screech had quickly quashed the idea. But thinking about Kramer had reminded him of the conversation he'd had with Yasiv regarding Drake. About how the DA was desperate to keep his job. About how he was seeking jail time for the dirty cops, instead of trying to just sweep all of the corruption under the rug.

With no other options, Screech had packaged the video of Captain Loomis assaulting Hanna and sent it anonymously to the DA. That had been a risk; threatening to go to the Times if the DA didn't do anything about it ASAP was borderline reckless.

But he couldn't wait—*Hanna* couldn't wait—for them to go through the proper channels and chain of custody and all that bullshit.

She'd be dead long before the slow-moving wheel of bureaucracy made it to the Loomis Estate.

Screech had been so deep in thought that he didn't even realize his phone had started ringing.

"Screech, your phone," Leroy informed him from the backseat.

Screech shook his head and focused on the screen. With a furrowed brow, he answered it.

"Sgt. Yasiv? What's going on?"

There was no answer.

"Yasiv? Everything okay?"

Screech initially thought that the line was dead, but when he listened closely, he realized that he could hear voices on the other end.

People barking commands.

And then, louder than the others, Yasiv's voice broke through.

"Yeah, DA says we're a go; arrest warrant for Captain Brandon Loomis. Intel has him at his Estate on the Upper East Side."

"Yasiv? Are you—"

"Ten, maybe fifteen minutes out."

"Are we going in hot?" another voice asked. It was then that Screech realized that Yasiv wasn't speaking to him.

And then he smiled. Yasiv couldn't update him directly, of course, but this 'accidental' phone call was just as good.

"Hot?" Yasiv shouted. "No, not hot. We're going in blazing. Strap up boys, it's gonna be a long night."

Chapter 63

DRAKE FELT AS IF HE'D stepped back in time to a place he'd never been.

Somehow, he'd transposed himself into the photograph that he'd seen in the Times, the one that showed a much younger Ken Smith in army fatigues, his arm wrapped around Raul's shoulder. In the background, he could see the sign for the *Iglesia de Liberacion*, complete with the symbol for ANGUIS Holdings.

Nothing had changed. More than thirty years had passed, and yet the sign was still there, as was the hut. Drake had to do a double-take to make sure that he hadn't somehow *become* Ken Smith.

Drake opened his eyes as wide as he could, trying to force away the exhaustion. It didn't work.

Dane suddenly turned to look at him. Then he nodded. There was no need for words now, the words had all been said.

Now was the time for action. Dane reached into the bottom of his backpack and pulled out two items. He handed one to Drake and took the other for himself.

Drake didn't know how many times he'd held a gun in his life. Dozens, probably even a hundred. But for some reason, this pistol felt different in his hand. Heavier, warmer, somehow even more deadly.

He swallowed hard. It wasn't the gun that was different, it was him.

Distracted as he was, Drake barely noticed when his brother rose out of his crouch and started to work his way around the back of the hut.

"No!" Drake hissed. He was suddenly struck with a sense of déjà vu that was so disorienting that he needed to shut his eyes for a moment.

He was torn between two worlds; part of his brain thought that he was back at Diego's hut, while the other half thought he was back in nineteen-eighty-four.

When Drake finally managed to shake this bizarre sensation and opened his eyes, his brother was gone.

"Fuck."

He ran his tongue across his blistered and cracked lips. He tasted blood, and this seemed to root him in the present.

By pressing his body as flat as possible by the edge of the clearing, Drake realized that he could almost render himself invisible. It wasn't such a bad thing, not being seen. Not being seen meant that you couldn't fuck up other people's lives.

Time flexed and bowed as he lay there. Drake existed in the uncomfortable space between waking and sleep, the space where dreams could come but you could never quite wake up from.

Mental purgatory, he thought. *That's what I suffer from. Mental purgatory.*

Shadows crossed the sun, tiny birds at first—hundreds of them, maybe even thousands—until they coalesced into larger forms. *Two* forms.

Two men, standing in front of the hut.

Drake blinked rapidly and forced his muscles to wake.

"Drake? I know you're out there," a voice hollered.

Dane? Is that Dane?

He still couldn't focus on the two figures. One was standing in front of the other, that much he could make out, but for some reason, his brain seemed incapable of separating the men into two discreet images.

"Drake, show yourself, or I'll kill him right here, right now."

It wasn't the words, but the cocking of a gun that finally helped clear Drake's mind.

His brother was standing in front, his head hung low. Behind him, a silver-haired man in fatigues pressed a gun to the back of Dane's head.

All his training, all his instincts, all his common sense told Drake to stay down, to stay out of sight.

But he'd gone thirty-five plus years not listening to his common sense, and even though that approach to life had gotten him here, to this place, old habits died hard.

"Dane!" Drake shouted as he rose to his feet.

Ken Smith turned in his direction and then nudged Dane forward several feet with the muzzle of the gun.

Drake raised his own pistol and aimed it at Ken.

"I'll kill you," he said hoarsely. "I'll fucking kill you."

Ken smirked.

"I knew you'd come," he said.

Drake tried desperately to line Ken's head up with the barrel of his gun, but it was hopeless. His hand kept moving, and the man's face was continually drifting in and out of focus. Under the best of circumstance, Drake would have had a hard time making the shot.

Under these circumstances? After not sleeping for two days, drinking only a teaspoon of water in the sweltering heat, and having the shakes from alcohol withdrawal?

Impossible. I'd hit Dane before I hit Ken.

And yet rage continued to build inside him. A rage so powerful that it caused his index finger to tighten on the trigger.

"I knew both of you would come."

Dane's own gun, which he'd been gripping this entire time, slipped from his hand and landed in the dirt by his feet.

"Predictable. Relentless, sure, but predictable."

The trees to Drake's right suddenly shook and a man stepped into the clearing.

The man's eyes darted from Ken to Dane, to Drake, and then back again.

What the fuck?

It was Raul.

Drake didn't know how this was possible, but it *was* Raul. The impish man was shirtless, his deeply tanned skin dripping with sweat and glistening in the sun. Over one shoulder was a large parcel wrapped in brown paper. The ends were sealed with red tape covered in the familiar snake eating an eyeball symbol.

The symbol for the Church of Liberation.

For ANGUIS Holdings.

Drake turned his head in the man's direction and blinked several times.

"Raul?" he barely managed to whisper. "How is this possible? How—"

And then Drake felt something cold press up against his temple and the blood in his arteries that fury had boiled froze in his veins.

Chapter 64

"ROBERT EAKIN THE THIRD, I know you're here!" Mandy shouted the second she stepped into the auction room. All eyes were suddenly on her, which was exactly what she wanted. "Where's Robert Eakin?"

People exchanged uncomfortable glances, all wondering who the feisty brunette in the sexy dress was.

When nobody gave Robert up, Mandy made her way directly to the center of the room.

"Where's Robert? Where's Robert Eakin?"

When once again nobody replied, she grabbed for the nearest man, a wiry fellow with dark hair, and pulled him close.

"You know Robert? Robert Eakin?"

The man was so startled that he didn't even bother pushing her away.

"Yeah, he's h-h-here somewhere," the man blubbered.

"Take me to him, take me to him now," Mandy demanded. In her periphery, she saw Veronica sneaking around to the other side of the room, moving seamlessly through the crowd whose eyes were all focused on her.

Moving toward the basement.

A man suddenly stepped into the room from the other side, nearly knocking into Veronica in the process. She slid out of his path just before they collided.

"Robert," Mandy said with a grin. "We have some business to discuss."

The man looked confused and his thick, bushy eyebrows rose up his forehead. But when he noticed that everyone's eyes were now on him, his face started turning red.

"Do I—do I know you?" He stammered, stepping into the room. Mandy let go of the man she'd interrogated and stepped toward Robert. His Adam's apple bobbed. "M-M-Mandy? What the hell—what the hell are you doing here?"

"We've got some business to discuss," she reiterated, placing her hands on her hips.

Robert's face transitioned from red to purple.

He mumbled something else, something incoherent, and was about to step forward when a large man with gray hair pushed by him.

"What the hell is going on here?"

Mandy smirked. She knew by the man's air of authority that this was the person in charge.

That this was Captain Brandon Loomis.

"I came here for Robert. He—"

Loomis snapped his fingers, interrupting her.

"Security, get this woman out of here," he ordered.

The security seemed to materialize out of thin air. They grabbed her arms and bent them behind her back, but Mandy didn't resist.

In fact, when she saw Veronica sliding behind Captain Loomis and making her way out of the room, her smile grew.

Chapter 65

"OR SHOULD I SAY, WE knew you'd come. Now, be a good boy, Drake, and put down your gun."

Drake's mind was swimming. He didn't need to see who was holding the gun to his temple to know who it was.

After all, it could only be one person. And that person was Wesley Smith.

It took him another moment to realize that this must have been Ken and Wesley's plan all along. Everything from putting Drake into lockup, to having Diego tell them where they were.

It was all to get both him and Dane together.

Ken must've seen something on his face change because his smirk grew into a full-fledged smile.

"Yeah, I knew you'd come after me, and I knew that when you got into trouble, Dane would come to the rescue. Just like he did at the Reynolds farm. Dane was supposed to die on that stupid yacht, but, in the end, I'm glad he didn't. This is better."

Movement out of the corner of his eye drew Drake's attention.

It was Raul—or, more appropriately, the man he *thought* was Raul. But while the man looked like Raul, he lacked his bristly mustache and the deep lines around his mouth. He was younger, was fitter.

It was Raul's son.

And with this realization, everything suddenly came into focus for Drake and he was met with a clarity that he hadn't felt since Clay's murder.

This was why Raul was so indebted to Ken, not because he rescued him from the drug lords who'd forced him to make their product, but because he'd saved his son.

"Put down the gun, Drake," Wesley Smith ordered.

But Drake didn't listen. He knew that the moment he lowered his weapon, both he and his brother were as good as dead.

Ken sighed heavily.

"I've grown tired of you, Drake. There was a time when I thought we could work together, that I could bring you into the fold, into ANGUIS like I did with Clay all those years ago. We could have used someone like you. If only you hadn't been so goddamn stubborn, maybe neither of us would have ended up here."

Clay... just the mention of his late friend's name caused Drake's entire body to thrum.

All of this was because of Clay.

"But here's the thing, Drake. Only one of us is getting out of this jungle. And it ain't gonna be you. It'll take some time to build up what you destroyed in New York, but rest assured, I will. After all, not all the rats went down with the ship. I still have people there, people who owe me. But most of all, I have the product."

Drake wasn't listening to Ken anymore. His mind was flipping forward from the time of Clay's murder. He'd gone rogue for a while, but then he'd been assigned a new partner, one who kept him grounded. And their first case...

His first case with Chase Adams was investigating the murder of a man who had been stripped naked, his arms and legs bound behind his back, a bloody butterfly painted on his pale flesh.

"Thomas Alexander Smith," he whispered. "The butterfly killer."

"What did you say?" Wesley snarled.

Drake shook his head slightly but stopped when the gun was jabbed painfully into his temple.

"Nothing," he grumbled.

"Put the gun down, Drake," Ken repeated, the smile now all but gone off his face. "It's over."

"No, you're going to tell me what you just said," Wesley ordered.

"Wes, let it—"

Wesley held his free hand up to his father, silencing him. Drake watched as Ken's lips twisted into a frown.

He wasn't a man who was used to being told what to do.

"Let him speak."

"I don't think—"

"Be quiet," Wesley snapped.

Ken's eyes went dark and Raul's boy slowly lowered the heavy package to the ground in anticipation of what was to come.

Drake suddenly recalled how Wesley had freaked out when he'd mentioned his name back beneath the diner. How the man had lost control and knocked him out.

"Jesus," he said softly. "You don't know, do you?"

"Know what?"

Drake sighed, and his eyes drifted to his brother's, to the emptiness within. They'd come so far but had regressed even further.

"You don't know about your brother, about Thomas, do you?" he said almost forlornly. "You don't know what your father did."

The pressure on his temple eased a little.

"This is bullshit," Ken said, a slight tremor creeping into his voice. "He's just making stuff up, trying to save himself.

Power... this is all about power, always has been.

Ken Smith and his son Wesley were cut from the same cloth, but Thomas wasn't. He was different.

Drake remembered the video that he'd gotten from Dr. Kruk, the one where Thomas spelled out this difference in no uncertain terms. How he didn't share his father's quest for power.

But Wesley sure as hell did.

"What did he do?" Wesley demanded.

"Wes, don't listen—"

"Shut up! Drake, tell me what he did!"

Drake took a deep breath and looked away from Dane.

"Your dad... your dad killed him, Wesley. Your dad killed your brother."

Chapter 66

BLOOD POOLED REPEATEDLY IN HANNA'S mouth and she had to hang her head to one side to let it leak out. The bottom of her tongue had been punctured, but she didn't think that nor the hole beneath her chin were fatal.

One thing was for certain, however, if Steffani returned, she wouldn't hesitate in delivering the final blow.

I have to get out of here, she thought. But it was a useless thought, one that had no bearing in reality. She couldn't move, she couldn't so much as stand, let alone get out of this place. And while there was some sort of commotion going on up above, she couldn't count on anybody coming to rescue her, either.

Hanna desperately glanced around looking for anything to help her out of her predicament, but she saw nothing. She was surrounded by stone and concrete walls. Her only chance was the single window up high above her.

A window that she couldn't possibly get to because she was strapped to a chair.

Panic returned.

I have to get out of here. I have to—

The door at the top of the staircase suddenly opened, but it wasn't thrown wide as Captain Loomis had previously done. This time it was opened just enough for a person to slip through before it was closed again.

Shrouded in near darkness, Hanna felt her heart start to race again, which only increased the amount of blood spilling to the floor.

"Don't kill me, please," she said, but her words were garbled by all the fluid in her mouth.

It's Steffani, she came down here to finish the job. To make sure that she killed me before whatever is going on upstairs got out of hand.

But as the figure approached, she saw that it was a man, not a woman. A man not nearly as large and imposing as Captain Loomis.

"Screech?" she said hopefully.

But it wasn't Screech; it was someone else.

"Mackenzie?"

The man nodded as he stepped into view.

"Shit, she stuck you good," he muttered. He pulled the white pocket square from his suit jacket and then gently grabbed her chin to inspect the damage.

Hanna had to pull back and spit to clear her mouth of blood.

"I'm going to put this under your tongue to try and stem the bleeding," Mackenzie informed her.

Hanna nodded and then lifted her tongue to allow him to jam the material inside her mouth.

Almost immediately, the pocket square started to soak up blood. And then, without another word, Mackenzie set about undoing the shackles on her wrists and ankles.

"Who are you?" Hanna tried to ask, but what with the fluid and the kerchief in her mouth, her words were unintelligible.

I'm a fixer... I'm good with my hands.

"Don't speak," he ordered. "We need to hurry."

Hanna waited, and less than a minute later, she let out a sigh as her wrists were freed. She instinctively rubbed the soreness from them, and then her ankles were free too. Mackenzie wrapped his arm around her waist and helped her to her feet. Then he tried to close her torn dress, but Hanna shook her head; that was the least of her worries.

All she cared about now was getting the fuck out of here before Steffani returned.

Mackenzie, sensing her fear, started towards the bottom of the stairs before suddenly stopping.

"What is it?" Hanna tried to say, but once again her words were muffled.

Mackenzie brought a finger to his lips and then pointed at the door.

Someone was trying to open it.

Hanna's eyes went wide, then Mackenzie moved his finger from the door to the window.

Without waiting for further instructions, she bolted over to it and Mackenzie followed.

Chapter 67

"IT'S TRUE," DRAKE SAID WITH a nod. "He arranged your brother's death, hooked him up with a psychiatrist who has a split personality disorder and a penchant for murder."

"Bullshit," Wesley snapped back.

He didn't know. Drake couldn't believe he hadn't seen this before. Wesley didn't know about any of this.

"Ask him," Drake demanded.

Wesley's eyes flicked over to his father's.

"Don't listen to any of this bullshit, he'll say anything to save his life. We got what we wanted, Wesley. We got both the Drake brothers. We can end this now and start to rebuild our empire, get back to where we were, back to New York. Everything's still in place. I've got people there, people that can get us out of this trouble. It'll take time, but—"

"Is it true?" Wesley demanded. "Did you get Thomas killed?"

Ken took a step back from Dane but kept the gun trained at the back of his head.

"No, of course, it isn't true. He was murdered by some psychopath… I had nothing to do with it."

"He's lying," Drake said. "Your brother had a video of your dad, of him talking about your business. He was going to send it to the press, and Ken couldn't allow that. So, he came up with an elaborate plan to get Thomas to see a psychiatrist, one who just happened to be someone Thomas terrorized as a teenager."

"He's talking out of his ass, Wesley. Let's get this over with," Ken said. But there was something in his voice now, something different. A hesitation, a tremor, maybe.

Or maybe Drake's mind was just fabricating this whole thing.

Maybe he died back when Wesley had first abducted him.

Maybe this was just his mental purgatory.

"You know who killed your brother?" Drake asked. Purgatory or not, he wasn't going to stop now.

"Yeah, Dr. Kruk."

"And you know his other name? His real name? Marcus Slasinsky?"

Wesley nodded.

"Yeah, I read about it. I know all about it."

"Then you know that I'm the one who caught the bastard, threw him in prison," Drake continued.

"And the one who let him back out again," Ken said quickly. But both Drake and Wesley ignored him.

"Don't you think it's strange that of all the psychiatrists in New York, your brother just happened to pick the one who'd assumed a new name, a person who he knew long ago?"

Wesley just stared.

"Who do you think paid for those sessions, Wesley? Come on, use your brain. And who do you think paid off the cops so that your brother wasn't prosecuted when he gave Marcus Slasinsky a nervous breakdown?"

Wesley still said nothing, but he swallowed audibly.

"Don't listen to—"

"Shut up," he said hoarsely.

A hint of a smile formed on Drake's lips. Wesley was on the edge and all he needed was one… final… push.

"But here's the kicker, Wesley," Drake continued slowly. "It was your dad who paid for Marcus Slasinsky to go to school, to become a psychiatrist. He planned your brother's murder long before he even made that tape."

"You did this," Wesley said softly. "You killed Thomas."

Ken's eyes went dark.

"And he'll kill you when you're no longer useful," Drake said. "He won't even hesitate."

Wesley suddenly pulled his gun away from Drake's temple and swung it around. He aimed it at his father.

"You did it! You killed him! You killed my brother, your son!" Wesley suddenly roared.

This was the tipping point.

Drake knew that it would come to this. He remembered Wesley from all those years ago, how he'd come to Thomas's wife's house, how he'd demanded that the woman stay quiet. Not because he was involved, but because he was hurting, he was furious. Wesley loved his brother, and in that way, he wasn't like his father.

All Ken had to do was continue to deny it, to stick to the refrain that this was all a coincidence, a desperate ploy for Drake to save his and Dane's lives.

But Ken couldn't do that. He couldn't do that because now he was being challenged, and like the alpha that he was, when the king of the jungle was threatened with being dethroned, he had to stand up for himself.

Power… it's about power now, and it always has been.

"Of course, I did," Ken yelled, his mouth twisting into a snarl. "I had to kill your brother because he was weak. He was going to bring me down, he was going to bring all of us… everything that we worked for. He was—"

There was a growl from Drake's left and in his periphery, he saw Wesley take a single step forward.

And then someone squeezed the trigger and all hell broke loose.

Chapter 68

WHILE MANDY WAS BEING HAULED away, Veronica slipped into the hallway. Screech hadn't given her much to go on, except for the fact that Hanna was being held in some sort of basement. The problem with that was, every door that she passed looked the same.

There was no telling which one led to the basement.

And now, with everybody moving in the opposite direction, toward the front of the Estate, it wouldn't be long before someone noticed her going against the grain.

But she wasn't giving up.

If this Hanna, whom she'd never met, was a friend of Screech and Drake? Well, then she was a friend of Veronica and Mandy.

She would do everything in her power to make sure that the girl left here alive.

Veronica tried the first door she passed but this led to an office. The second was some sort of yoga room.

"Shit," she swore under her breath. Hanna would die from old age before she ever found her by going door to door.

Just as she was about to consider other options, she noticed a flicker of color up ahead. It was the swirl of a dress as someone took a left near the end of the hallway.

And, like Veronica, she was heading *away* from the front of the building.

Pressing her back up against the wall, Veronica hurried after the woman.

This better lead to Hanna, Veronica thought as she took several different hallways. *Otherwise, I'll be the one dying of old age trying to find my way out again.*

The woman stopped in front of a door with a heavy-duty electronic lock on it. She raised her head and looked around; Veronica barely managed to duck out of sight in time.

Staying as still as possible, Veronica heard a beep, followed by the unmistakable sound of a door opening.

Without even looking, Veronica pushed off the wall and spun around the corner. And then she hauled ass toward the now closing door.

She almost missed it. But she slipped at the last second on the polished floors. This caused her left foot to shoot and, as luck would have it, become wedged between the door and the frame.

After taking a moment to catch her breath, Veronica slid inside, letting the door close silently behind her.

Then she stood at the top of the stairs, staring down at a woman and an empty chair.

Chapter 69

NONE OF THE ANXIETY THAT coursed through Screech's veins dissipated even after the sound of sirens filled the night air. Until he saw Sgt. Yasiv with Captain Loomis and his daughter Steffani in handcuffs, dragging them both away, he would remain on edge.

"Come on, come on," he mumbled, tapping his foot, which caused the gun on his lap to bounce up and down.

People were being ushered out of the front of the house by security, and they looked none too happy about it. But it was the woman who exited out the back that held his attention.

Screech's first thought was that it was Hanna, and he felt his tapping slow. But the dress was different, and this woman's hair was longer than his partner's.

Without thinking, he opened the car door and started to rise.

"Uhh, Screech?" Leroy asked from the backseat. Screech ignored him; his eyes were locked on the woman who was hurrying across the yard.

It wasn't Hanna, but it was definitely someone he knew.

Someone that he had to speak to.

His legs moved as if by their own accord, carrying him across the street and over the short fence. The guests and security were so concerned with seeing people off the property, that they never noticed him trying to get *on* the Estate grounds.

"Jasmine?" Screech said in a strange tone. "Is that you?"

The woman stopped cold and then spun around to look at him.

It was indeed Jasmine. Jasmine Cuthbert, mother to Drake's child.

And she looked... *terrified*.

Her eyes darted down to the gun in his hand, the gun that Screech hadn't realized he'd been carrying, and her face went a stark white.

"Screech? What the... what the hell are you doing here?"

Chapter 70

AT FIRST, DRAKE DIDN'T KNOW who fired the gun, he only knew that he hadn't been the target.

But when a crimson eye appeared on Ken Smith's forehead just above his left eyebrow, he knew. Ken's mouth went slack as if in complete shock, for a second it looked like he was about to say something, to admonish Wesley for daring to do such a thing, but the man was mortal, after all. Ken Smith staggered, then fell to his knees.

Wesley Smith burst into sobs to his left, but Drake knew better than to wait for the man to collect himself. He turned the gun that had previously aimed at Ken on the man and fired three shots in rapid succession.

While hitting Ken would have been impossible from his range, Drake had no problem targeting a man three or four feet away, even if his eyes were still locked on his brother's.

The bullets peppered Wesley Smith's side, making three holes in a dice pattern.

The man grunted, but unlike his father who fell silently on his face, Wesley cried out and dropped to the ground, immediately curling protectively around his wounds.

Drake, still stunned by what had happened, simply watched the man for a moment. It wasn't that he felt bad, not really; Wesley Smith was responsible for the deaths of many people, not least the addicts that he sold tainted heroin to.

It was just that he couldn't believe that both Smiths were now dead. After chasing Ken for—

"Don't let him suffer," Dane said, suddenly appearing by his side. Drake looked at his brother as he raised his gun and shot the man in the side of the head.

He fell still instantly.

Something inside Drake lurched and he vomited yellow bile onto the dirt. Having not eaten or had anything to drink for some time, his second bout proved even less productive. As he dry heaved, he realized that Dane had taken off, sprinting toward the hut.

Drake let him go. It was over now. The nightmare was finally over.

The Skeleton King and his minions were dead.

"Let go of me!"

Drake raised his head and wiped the tears from his eyes.

His brother hadn't bolted for the jungle to live out his days in solitude as Drake had thought or hoped.

Instead, he'd gone for the young man. Visibly shaken by the violence, he didn't react quickly enough; Dane grabbed him by the waist and held him tight.

"No," Drake groaned, standing up straight and raising his pistol. Dane didn't seem to notice him. He was too busy trying to get the young man to stop squirming so that he could deliver a kill shot.

"No!"

Dane, brow furrowed, looked over at him this time.

"This is Raul's son," Dane proclaimed.

Drake didn't need an explanation; he knew who this was.

"Don't do it, Dane," Drake pleaded. "He's just a kid, let him go."

Dane shook his head. When the boy's struggles intensified, he snaked an arm around his neck and started to squeeze.

"If we don't take him out, he'll come for you. He'll spend his whole life looking for the man who put his father behind bars and killed his mentor. His suffering will be immense."

Drake shook his head.

"You know this to be true, Drake," Dane said in his strange, flat affect. "You know what happens to a person when they lose someone they love. The suffering is all-encompassing. It is everything."

Drake lowered his gun and breathed deep.

What Dane was saying was true, of course; it was true of him when he'd lost Clay, and it was true of his brother when he'd lost Ray.

Everyone is suffering.

His eyes fell on Wesley's head and the pool of blood surrounding it.

And yet Raul's son was just a young man. He didn't choose the life he was born into, he didn't choose any of this.

"Let's end this now, Drake. One shot and it's all over. Painless. No more suffering."

He didn't choose this life, it was given to him.

Drake wiped the tears from his eyes and leveled his gun at his brother once more.

"Let him go, Dane."

Dane shook his head and tightened his grip around the man's throat. He was struggling to breathe now.

"Please."

The boy didn't choose this life, but it wasn't up to them to choose whether or not he should continue living it.

"Please, Dane, I'm begging you, just let him go."

If he wanted to come for Drake, so be it; Drake would be ready. That would be *his* choice.

"Dane…"

Dane just blinked at him with those cold, hard eyes.

At that moment, Drake knew that his brother wouldn't let go—that he would never let go.

There was suffering in this world, Dane was right about that. And this was the end. Just not for Raul's son.

"Please," Drake said, tears spilling down his cheeks now. "Please, Dane."

But even as he uttered those words, Drake was already stepping forward and pulling the trigger.

Chapter 71

VERONICA SLID SILENTLY DOWN THE stairs.

The woman with her back to her was staring at the empty chair. She'd since slipped something from her dress and was now holding it in her hand.

A growl drifted up to Veronica, and then the woman hurried over to the open window and peered out.

"Shit!"

She whipped around and for the first time, noticed Veronica standing on the landing. Only in the darkness, she didn't realize who it was.

"I don't know how you got out, Hanna, but I'm going to enjoy killing you."

As if to emphasize her point, Steffani strode forward with the knife-like object held out in front of her. That's when Veronica reached into her clutch and pulled a weapon of her own.

"I'm not Hanna," she said as she moved to meet her. "And I think you're going to need something bigger than a chopstick to kill me."

Veronica stepped into the moonlight and Steffani Loomis's eyes went wide.

"Wh-what? Who are—"

Veronica pressed the button on the side of the Taser and the leads sparked to life. Then she drove the points into Steffani's sternum.

Chapter 72

"**WHAT ARE _YOU_ DOING HERE?**" Screech shot back.

"I'm... I'm..." Jasmine just shrugged and appeared to give up.

Screech grunted.

Where the fuck are you, Drake? Where are you?

Sensing his indecision, Jasmine suddenly found her tongue again.

"I've got information on all them. I can help you put them away, Screech. That's all I ever wanted. I only wanted —"

And that's when Screech noticed a second figure on the lawn behind Jasmine.

"I knew it; Steffani said that she could trust you, that we needed you, but I knew it. I knew that after Clay was murdered, you'd come back to haunt us," Captain Loomis said as he stepped from the shadows, his eyes drifting from Jasmine to Screech.

"You?" he said with a quasi-chuckle. "You're really turning into being a real pain in the ass, you know that? Drake's little fuckin' minion." The sirens were louder now, which meant that Loomis needed to almost shout to be heard. "I'll be back, I'll come back stronger. You mark my words."

He started to move away from the Estate toward the edge of the forest when Screech raised his gun.

Captain Loomis stopped.

"What? You're going to shoot me now? Boy, you don't have the balls to shoot me. I'm a war hero and I'm unarmed. You're not going to shoot me on my own lawn."

Screech shook his head and turned his gaze skyward, once again wishing that Drake were here, that Drake would tell him what to do.

"That's what I thought," Captain Loomis said as he started toward the treeline once more.

It wasn't the taunts, the threats, or even the insults that got to Screech.

No, it was something else.

It was what Captain Loomis had done to Hanna in the basement. Hanna, who was now probably lying in a pool of her own blood.

That and Screech thought that there was a high probability that the man really would get away with all of this.

A snake… no, a worm—cut the head off a worm, and it'll keep living.

"You shouldn't have hit her," Screech muttered.

Captain Loomis's eyes suddenly widened.

"What did you say, boy? What did you—"

And then a new sound joined the cacophony of sirens.

The sound of the gun in Screech's hand going off.

Chapter 73

SGT. HENRY YASIV STARED AT his computer monitor as the video played out. He'd watched it a half-dozen times before, maybe even more. He'd watched alone, he'd watched it with Detective Dunbar, and he'd watched it with the DA.

To him, it clearly looked like Captain Brandon Loomis implicated his daughter; *multiple* times, in fact. But with the revered Army Captain now buried on the Loomis plot and Hanna staying out of the media spotlight, there was no way to corroborate what he'd said. And, with no audio, a defense attorney would shred each and every lip-reading expert they put on the stand.

For all the DA's bravado, for all his claims about wanting to put an end to the corruption, he was still afraid to lose.

The reality was, Loomis wasn't like Raul, or Palmer, or even Ken Smith; he was a war hero, and the people of New York took this seriously.

As they should.

But that didn't change the fact that his entire family was corrupt and heavily involved in the importing of heroin into the city, amongst other things.

Yasiv knew that past deeds did not make up for present failures, as past failures didn't abolish present deeds. Case in point Damien Drake. Yasiv had done all he legally could to try and convince others that he deserved a second chance, a clean slate.

After all, Drake and his team were the ones to bring the drug kingpins of New York to their knees.

Only Yasiv couldn't deliver the death blow.

"Fuck," he grumbled, rubbing his eyes. He needed a cigarette and badly.

"I'm going for a smoke," he told Dunbar as he backed away from his computer.

Yasiv made his way outside and lit up. He inhaled deeply, enjoying the way that the smoke filled his lungs and the nicotine rushed into his bloodstream and then onto his brain.

It had been a long, long six weeks. And something told him that this wasn't quite over yet.

"Sgt. Yasiv?" A female voice said.

Yasiv took another drag and turned toward the voice. It belonged to a woman with long dark hair and large sunglasses that covered most of her face. It was dusk, and the lighting was poor, but she looked familiar to him somehow.

"Yeah?" Yasiv asked, his hand slipping inadvertently to the butt of his gun. He didn't sense danger from the woman, but something was amiss.

"I was told you could be trusted. This is for you," she said handing over a large envelope that was bursting at the seams. Yasiv looked at the package without taking it, then stared intently at the woman.

It took him a full ten seconds before he put a name to the face.

"Jasmine? Jasmine Cuthbert?"

The woman's expression didn't change.

"Take it. It'll help."

As soon as Yasiv took the package, she spun and started to move quickly away from 62nd precinct.

"Jasmine! Wait!"

The woman didn't turn.

"Wait! I—"

Jasmine walked around to the driver's side of a black Volkswagen and got behind the wheel.

"Shit," Yasiv swore. He flicked his cigarette and ran after her. Even while he knocked loudly on the passenger window, Jasmine just stared straight ahead, hands on the wheel, clearly debating whether she should just leave. In the end, she succumbed to his persistence and rolled down the window. "Jasmine, I can... I can help you. Whatever's going on, let me help you. *Please.*"

Jasmine shook her head.

"You can't help me," she said. "You won't see me again, Sgt. Yasiv. Just know this; whatever you read in that file, whatever you think about me, know that I did it for him; for *them.*"

Yasiv scrunched his nose.

"For who? Jasmine, what are you talking about? You did what for who?"

But the woman had already rolled up the window and had put the car into drive. As she pulled away from the curb, Yasiv found himself staring through the rear windshield.

Tucked into a rear facing baby seat was a boy with bright blue eyes.

It was Drake's son. Sadness welled in Yasiv, and he stayed in that same spot until the car had long since blended in with the others.

What the hell was that all about?

As he made his way back inside the precinct, Yasiv started to open the folder, more confused than when he'd left for a smoke.

The first image was of Jasmine. She was younger in the photo with flushed cheeks and red lips. In her hand was a brick of heroin. Beside her was skid full of brown packages wrapped in red tape.

"What's that?" Dunbar hollered.

Yasiv swallowed hard and quickly tucked the picture into his pocket. Then he reached inside the envelope and pulled a handful of the photographs out.

The first was of Steffani Loomis shaking Horatio Dupont's hand. The next also included Steffani, only this time she was alone, her index finger aimed at a giant barrel of white powder.

"Jesus," he whispered.

"What? Yasiv, what is that? Love letter?"

Yasiv ignored Dunbar and went to the round table in the center of the room. There were several documents piled on top of it, but he swept these onto the floor without even looking at them.

"Hey! What the hell—"

But when Dunbar saw the contents of the folder—the hundreds of implicating photographs—he fell silent.

"This is… this is it." Dunbar raised his head to look at him, a huge smile on his face. "Yasiv, this is it, man. This is what we need to put that bitch away! Fuck… this is *it!*"

And then, for the first time in a long time, Yasiv found himself smiling along with Detective Dunbar.

Yeah, he thought. *This* is *it.*

While Dunbar started to peruse the photos, Yasiv pulled a worn sheet of paper out of his pocket. He scooped a pen off the table and then drew a line through the final name on the list.

This is the end of ANGUIS Holdings.

Epilogue

"I'LL GET IT," SCREECH ANNOUNCED, rising to his feet.

"Are you sure that isn't the butler's job?" Leroy asked with a grin.

Screech shook his head and pulled the door open.

He was surprised to find a delivery man struggling to hold onto a large, rectangular package on the other side.

"What's this?"

The man popped his bubble-gum.

"Delivery for DSLH?"

It sounded like a question, but Screech was fairly certain that it was a statement.

"Yeah, but what is it?"

The man shrugged and cracked his gum again.

"No idea. You gotta sign here, and here, and here. You can sign for DSLH, right?"

Screech looked down at the lettering on the frosted glass.

He nodded.

"Sure can."

He scribbled his initials on the electronic pad that the delivery man thrust at him from his hip, and then took the package.

"What the hell is that?" Leroy asked as he brought it inside.

"Ask the butler," Screech replied.

He grabbed an X-Acto knife from his desk drawer and then carefully cut away the brown paper.

"It's a painting," Screech said.

Leroy hovered over his right shoulder.

"Looks like a bunch of dots to me."

"Yep, to me too."

"Is there a note? Who is it from?"

Screech found a small square of paper tucked into the frame. He read it out loud.

"*Consider this your payment – Greta Armatridge.*"

Screech rolled his eyes and crumpled the note into a ball.

"What the hell does that mean?"

"It means that Hanna just got her bonus, that's what it means."

"What? What—"

Screech's phone started to ring, and he held a finger up to Leroy while he answered it.

"Hello?"

"Stephen? Stephen, it's Roger."

Leroy mouthed the words who is it, and Screech shrugged.

"Who?"

"Roger Schneiderman."

Shit.

With everything that had happened, Screech had forgotten all about the lawyer.

"Sorry, Roger, I was—"

"So, I, uhh, I haven't received payment for the retainer. It's been a while since we last spoke."

Screech dipped his head to one side.

"Yeah, I'm sorry about that. I'll write a check—"

"It's been a good two months, Stephen."

Screech was about to apologize again when his wandering gaze fell on the lettering he'd put on the office door.

DSLH Investigations. Drake, Screech, Leroy, and Hanna Investigations.

"You know what, Roger? I don't think I'm going to make that payment."

"Wh-what? Stephen, I know that Drake isn't there now, but if he ever comes back, you're going to need—"

"Naw, I don't think he will. Thanks for your help, Roger, but I don't think I'm going to need you anymore."

Screech hung up before the man could argue his way out of it. He tapped the dull side of the knife on his hand a few times while he continued to stare at the lettering on the door.

"Umm… you gonna elaborate on that call?"

"Nope."

Screech walked over to the door and opened it. Then he lowered himself and sat cross-legged on the floor.

He knew that Leroy was watching him, but Screech didn't care. He had to do this.

Drake had left them, and he wasn't coming back. It was about time that they took his name off the door.

Screech was in the process of removing the *D* from *DSLH* when a hand came down on his shoulder and he jumped.

His first thought was that it was Drake, that the man was going to be frowning at him, telling him to pour him a drink and stop wrecking his door, but it wasn't him. It was a man that he didn't recognize, a handsome man with dark hair and a strong jaw covered with the beginnings of a beard.

"Can I help you?" Screech asked, tightening his grip on the X-Acto blade.

"Can I help you? No, I'm pretty sure that it's the other way around."

The man started to reach into his pocket and Screech tensed. When he pulled out a business card, Screech relaxed.

"What the hell is this?" he asked, taking the card.

Hart Investigator, the card read, then beneath that, *Mackenzie Hart, PI.*

"Drake's gone, Screech, and you can't do this on your own. You need my help. Why don't you and your team come work for me?"

Screech rose to his feet, but the man held his ground.

"Who are you? And how the hell do you know my name?"

The man shrugged and tucked his hands into his pockets.

"Like I said, you can't do this on your own. It's a dangerous place out there and when people know things about you, they can use it against you. Think about it. Come work for me."

With that, the man turned and headed down the hallway.

"Hey? *Hey!*"

The man just kept on walking.

"You've got my card. I'll be in touch."

Screech was looking down at the card when Hanna emerged from the bathroom and made her way over to him.

"Who was that? Tell me it was a client. *Please* tell me that was a client."

Her voice was still a little off due to the stitches in her tongue, and her face was bruised, but her sarcasm hadn't faded.

Screech took one final look down the hall before he slipped the business card into his pocket.

"Nobody; that was nobody," he said dully. "By the way, a package arrived for you. It's on my desk."

"Really?"

"Yeah, really."

Hanna glanced down at the mess that Screech was making of the door. He thought she was going to say something about it, but instead, she just continued inside.

Before making it to her desk, however, she turned back to face him.

"Hey, Screech, I've got a question for you."

"Yeah, what is it?"

"What do you do if you step on a land mine?"

Screech made a face.

"Hanna, I don't have time for—"

"Standard procedure is to jump fifty feet and spread over a large area."

Screech stared at her for a moment, blinked once, twice, then broke into laughter.

***

Drake thought that the sunset in the Colombian jungle was the most beautiful that he would ever see.

He was wrong.

Watching the sun bow its glowing head in the Virgin Gorda trumped that one by a large margin. The light reflecting off the ocean was like a blanket made of velvet color. It was so entrancing that he sank into his chair, transfixed by its entire descent.

Even after the sun was gone, Drake watched the moon take its place, casting its blue shards of ethereal light down on the world. After a while, it became too difficult to discern reality from reflection.

It was as if his world had once again been flipped upside down.

"Mr. Drake, sir?"

Drake wiped the tears from his eyes.

"Yeah, Kevin? What's up?"

"I was wondering if you'd like something to drink?"

Drake turned to look at the man, but he didn't see Kevin the bartender. Instead, he saw a younger version of Dane. His brother's features were full of hope and desire and aspiration, as most young people's faces are.

It was his brother's face before that fateful summer at Ray Reynolds's farm.

It was his face before the suffering had begun.

"Drake? Are you okay?"

Dane Drake's face vanished.

"Yeah, I don't know," he said softly. "I don't know if I'll ever be okay."

"I'm sorry… is there anything I can do?"

Drake turned his eyes away from Kevin and back to the ocean and the reflected moon.

"Yeah, I think there is something you can do. I think I'll have a drink. You have any Johnny Blue?"

END

Author's Note

THIS IS THE END; THE end of Drake's personal journey into his soul.

I love Drake and hope that one day he will return to New York City. Because even though Ken Smith and ANGUIS Holdings are gone, New York is a big city with big city problems, a city that can use a man like Drake. A man who tries his best to do right, a man who is relentless, determined, and unforgiving. He's not perfect—far from it—but who is?

I love Drake and I hope you love him, too.

So long, dear friend.

Best,
Patrick
Montreal, 2019

Printed in Great Britain
by Amazon

75831473R00156